Shewolf
In Paradise

By Janet Y. Williams

This book is a work of fiction. Names, characters, places and incidents are products of the author's imagination or are used factiously. Any resemblance to actual events or locales or persons, living or dead, is entirely coincidental.

Copyright © Janet Y. Williams (The Bahamas)

All rights reserved, including the right to reproduce this book or portions thereof in any form whatsoever.

Dedicated to all my freaky friends and family who I know will enjoy the reading. Much love to you all.

1

When you get older, you tend to cut through all the bullshit and get straight to the point. There is no need to beat around the bush, with this in her mind, she watched her prey as he entered her office. He had no idea what was going through his boss' mind as she sat panty less behind her desk.

"Good day, Ms. Hannah," he said in this deep, husky voice. Every time he spoke to her, his voice sent shivers and goosebumps up and down her spine.

"Good day to you too, Shawn. What have you done with the project I assigned you to?" eyebrow raised, as she watched him adjust his manhood to take a seat opposite her.

As he brings her up to speed, all she is thinking about is how to get him naked. Shawn, became fully aware of the fact that she was watching rather than listening to him. He doesn't know how to react, so he just continues with his briefing.

Katrina, knows that there is something extraordinary about, Shawn. No man has ever peeked her interest the way he does. His innocence is not only sexually appealing but also appeals to her animalistic side.

She has had countless dreams about making him her mate. And as she is well aware of, once he is her mate he will have to be her mate for life. But, Katrina's not sure if he can handle who she truly is. For you see, Katrina, is one of a few remaining female lycans, and she has lived longer than most because of the strict measures she has taken to stay safe and alive.

All her life she has searched for her life's mate and never found him until now. Yes, she knows what it is like to take a man to bed, none has ever fully satisfied her the way she knows Shawn will. For some strange reason she is always aware of his presence. His scent is more than an arousal for her. Shawn's mere presence caused her to stop and just focus on him and him only. While he is a distraction, he is highly intelligent man with a chiseled face, that emits sensual and sexual appeal for her. His boy reminds her of the lycan that turned her. Not overly muscular, well developed and well maintained.

Katrina, keeps her stare firmly on Shawn, knowing that it is making him uncomfortable. But, she also notices his arousal, has she walks from behind her desk, where her short skirt has ridden up her fit thighs. She is very pleased by seeing his cock getting hard, as he watches her movements.

Nervously, Shawn, continues by asking, "How would you like to proceed with the purchase and renovation of the property?"

Katrina stops and asks, "Can you see yourself living there, in all that beauty and seclusion?"

He is stunned and fascinated by her question, because in his mind's eye he can see them both naked and roaming the island, making love at a whim wherever and however they wanted to without fear of interruption. He shakes himself back to reality when she touches his shoulder lightly.

"Yes, of course I can. It is just so magnificently beautiful," is his quick response.

Katrina, laughs temptingly and says, "Book the hotel and flight arrangements for a week's stay for two."

Just the thought of having him alone for seven days has Katrina's female juices flowing.

She had plans alright and she knew just how she was going to execute every one of them.

Shawn, went home of a long grueling day, but he was too excited to sleep. Just imagining what it would be like to finally be alone with Katrina. He has had nights where he had dreamt of making mad, passionate love to her in a tropical paradise and now that dream may become a reality.

Katrina on the other hand relaxes in a hot bath with a glass of chardonnay, and plotting in her head how she will seduce Shawn. He should prove an easy target for her. She has after all hunted and conquered many men, but she will have to approach this one in a whole new way.

She realizes that she could fall madly in love with Shawn and that may be a problem. While she wants and needs a mate, can he truly live up to being a lycan or will she allow him to remain just a mortal man? She already knows the answer to these questions, she will have to turn him in order to get what she wants. With the warm water around her, she is more aroused by just the idea of turning him. Her breathing becomes shallow has she pulls on her nipples making them hard as pebbles. She can feel the heat of passion building in her as one of her hands makes its way down between her thighs. Katrina finds herself throbbing with desire for a man she has yet to feel physically. Her fore finger rubs her clit till it's hard, erect and throbbing. With her middle finger rubbing up and down on the swollen, throbbing lips of a pussy that has not felt a man's touch in more than three years. Her hips arch up to meet her fingers as she plunges two of them deep into her cock starved pussy. Her motion speeds up to a rhythm to some unheard beat. Her heart beats faster as her fingers probe deeper into her wanton pussy. She is one the verge of a miraculous orgasm, unlike any she has had in years. As she cums and collapses into the warm bath water, she can vividly see Shawn, standing before in all his manly glory. But, she knows he is miles away thinking of her.

But what Katrina didn't know was the fact that Shawn, while not an animal of the night like herself, he was another form of creature of the night. For you see he is what they call a soul traveler, meaning his soul could travel without his body going with it. So, when she thought she saw him in her bathroom, he actually was there. He loved his gift and always used it wisely, but tonight he was a bit careless, because she saw him.

While, yes he was miles away, he was always in her bathroom watching her pleasing herself. The more he watched, the more aroused he got. He could smell her female essence; to the point he could almost taste it. He was still stroking himself and seeing the sight of Katrina climaxing in such a beautiful and mysterious way. Shawn, didn't know nor understand why he had such a strong attraction for her, but he couldn't think straight until he relieved himself and soon. So as he stood before his floor length mirror, he continues stroking the biggest hard on that he has had in three years. His rhythm speeds up the same way hers did, as he becomes more excited and aching for a release. He is imagining what it would feel like to be inside of her. To feel her pussy walls squeeze him has he slides in and out of her. To feel her body, move in rhythm with his. To hear her moan as she becomes more aroused and as her body prepares to climax. To hear her call his name as she climaxes hot, wet and hard around his cock. All these images and feelings pushes him over the edge of sanity into a wild a frenzied explosion of sights smells and sounds. He cums hard and ejaculates on his mirror, his vision is blurred and he collapses on the floor where he sleeps.

The following morning it all seems to be business as usual for them both, until they cross each other's paths in the hallway. Katrina can smell him before he banks the corner and she likes the surprised look on his face.

"Good day Ms. Hannah. I got the information you asked for and will forward them via email to you," he says, as he takes her in inch by gorgeous inch. Remembering what she looked like naked and fully exposed.

"No need to forward them to me, Shawn," she smiles with her eyebrow raised and watching his breathing change and hearing his heart rate increase. "I was just on my way to your office to see how far you had gotten. I'll walk back with you so we can discuss and make final arrangements."

She laughs at the emotions that fast forward over his face, from fright to excitement and finally to arousal. Katrina, can sense and see that he loves the idea of having her only, but she can't understand the fear that lies just beneath his 'I got it together' persona. But, she knows that in time she will learn everything and more about her soon to be mate.

Shawn, stands there in awe of a woman he more than desires and yearns to be with. Not until she calls his name does he realize he was just standing there dreaming.

"Aaah, Shawn, don't you think we should finish our discussion in your office," she's elated to see the reaction she has on him.

"Oh yes ma'am," he responds as he reels himself in.

"Good, because I thought I may have to spank you to get your attention," she smirks and walks away with him following next to her.

Katrina has no idea of the impact her words have on him. But his plan is to soon show her that he is more than willing to be either slave or master, it will all depend upon her and her wishes.

Shawn can't help but watch her as she walks in her usual sultry manner. He makes his desire for her to grow even more. With each passing encounter it gets harder for him to hide his arousal for his female boss. His imagination is always running wild when it comes to her and how she views him.

Little does he know that while he is deep in thoughts about her, Katrina is also deep in thoughts about him. Like what would his reaction be if or when, she shows him who she truly is. Also, if he would reject her and refuse to become her lifetime mate. All these and more are running through her head, but at the time she watches how he's moving. Long strong strides, with a well-built upper body, that promises to be beautiful when exposed. Katrina knows that without a doubt Shawn can and will provide the pleasure she much desires from more, but that is not all she will require from him.

As they approach his office door, Shawn's secretary, Simone, walks over with a savage and jealous look in her eyes. She has been lusting after her boss from the first moment she saw him. And boy did she do her research on him, more internet, background checks, financial records and more. Simone, promised that she would let no female ever take him away from her. Even if it means killing one of the world's most powerful female CEO's.

Simone Carlton, has mastered her crafts and skills in witchcraft for more than a hundred years and for the life of her she doesn't understand why none of her potions or spells seem to work on Shawn. Now here along comes Miss Bigshot CEO Katrina, she knows that Katrina will be a major challenge. Not only is she filthy rich, she has beauty and brain, and forever lusted after by men of all walks of life.

"Good afternoon, Ms. Hannah. Mr. Kenny, you have several messages from a real estate agent in the Bahamas by the name of Mr. Garvin Knowles. He wishes to speak to you as soon as humanly possible," she says with a sideways glance at their overall boss. Shawn, can more than feel but sees the tension building in his secretary.

"Thank you, Simone. Get him on the phone, I am sure Ms. Hannah, would like to hear what he has to say." Order given, he leads Katrina into his office, where he gently closes the door behind him. He knows that doing this will add insult to injury for Simone. He knows of Simone, dreams of grandeur of both of them together, but he can't phantom the idea of being with a witch, not even for a great fucking session. He sighs and moves toward his desk, where Katrina as taken it upon herself to admire the view from behind his chair.

"I never know how to deal with people, who believe that they are entitled to my affection, time and attention. Shawn, how can you put up with a secretary that disrespects you in front of, not just your boss, but hers as well." With her signature expression of a raised right eyebrow and a sexy smirk, she turns awaiting a reply from him. All he can do at this point, is to stare blankly out his office window.

"Well she is excellent at her job and she keeps me on my toes," was the only reply he could come up with, all of which was true.

"Mmm I see. I wonder if that's all the services she provides you with."

Just as Shawn, was about to respond to this statement, his phone rang and Simone informed him that she had Mr. Knowles on the line. Saved by the bell was Katrina's, reaction when she saw the ruthless expression on Shawn's face.

"Please put him through," he said. "Good afternoon Mr. Knowles. How are things looking for the completion of the said and transfer of deeds?"

"I have the deeds as we speak. Will you and Ms. Hannah, be travelling as planned next week? We can finalize everything else then."

"Yes. You can expect us first thing Monday morning, to be in your office to sign off on the deeds and make the final payment," Shawn told Mr. Knowles.

After he was done, he looked up and smiled at Katrina. Her heart stopped and her breathe was blown away, at the sheer beauty in his smile. There was nothing fake nor fraudulent look that lay in that smile, it was genuine pleasure that she got from it.

He was pleasantly surprised by the expression on Katrina's face. He had never seen her radiant beauty, the way he did now. She was not just powerful in business, but the tailored suit she wore, showed off a well-built body and chiseled legs that went on forever. Her breasts were slightly exposed, showed tanned well developed chest with a birthmark faint above the right breast. Shawn, imagined himself buried in them on a cold day, all warm and comfy.

"Well I have some great news, Ms. Hannah. That was the real estate agent and he has confirmed final purchase and the deeds are in his possession until we arrive to sign off on them. Also, all the travel arrangements have been made, we leave on Sunday. We will be staying at a little bed and breakfast on the island next to the cay that you are buying." She loved the fire, passion and excitement that she saw in his eyes.

Katrina was even more drawn and attracted to him. The desire she has for him; she knows will continue to build with time. Plus, she is thinking of a way to extend their time together.

"Great, and as a form of celebration let me treat you to an awesome dinner to any restaurant of your choice. So name the time and the place." She watched his body go through a strange transformation as Simone entered the office unannounced.

'Oh why did she have to come in here just when I was about to answer Kat.' Shawn wonders as he just sits and stares at his secretary. She has never reacted this way before and he thinks that it may have something to do with the weird things he keeps finding in his office. Or, it could be the length of time that Kat, his imaginary pet name for his boss, was in his office. After all he never had female visitors, work or personally, visit him.

Simone was rigid with anger. 'Who does she think she is taking up all his time, doesn't she know he has work to do? Or are they doing more than just work?' These thoughts and more ran through her head as she sat at her desk, getting angrier by the minute. Simone, couldn't take it anymore, she had to know what they were doing. She got up and burst through the office door, but stopped sudden not knowing what excuse to use for the rude intrusion.

To Katrina this was here cue to leave. She graciously told them both good day and walked out the office.

3

Back in her own office, Katrina, leans against the door in a daydream state. She is so caught up in her thoughts that she barely notices that she has a visitor. When she does realize his presence, she composes herself and asks him who he is.

"Sorry for the interruption to your day, Ms. Hannah, my name is Jerome McPhee. I am a private investigator. My employer has hired me to do a background check on one of your employees." He stated plainly.

Katrina is shocked, because she herself does background checks on all her employees.

"Please have a seat, Mr. McPhee."

He sits in the guest seat opposite her desk. He is taken aback by her beauty and obvious appearance of not just brains but strength. He was taken so much by her that he almost forgot the reason he was even in her office. Jerome had to pull himself out of the haze and back to reality.

He begins by telling her that his employer was seeking some information on Simone Carlton. The more he spoke, the more curious Katrina became.

According to Mr. McPhee, his employer at one time was dating Simone and was now seeking her location, because as time went on he realized that she wasn't who she said she was. So, now he was checking over all the information that was given to him by his employer and that's how he ended up here, in Katrina's, office.

While she sits and listens to the detective, she realizes that she always had some suspicions about Simone from the moment she had laid eyes on her.

As Mr. McPhee continues, Katrina, knows that she as to get as much information from him as she can. She allows him to finish talking and once he is done it is now her time to question him.

"Mr. McPhee, being one of the world's wealthiest and most powerful women, I myself take certain security measures. Also, being a CEO of a conglomerate of companies worldwide, I have had all my employees investigated and I have found discrepancies in the investigation I had done. But, I have someone still checking into her background as well. Should you care to exchange and compare notes, I will gladly have a copy of her file made up and sent to you."

"Thank you, Ms. Hannah, that will be most appreciated, here is the hotel I am staying at while I am here. Feel free to contact me at any time whether day or night." Smiling Jerome, got up, shook her hand and left.

Katrina, sat with her back to her office door staring out of the window. The next move she would make before her trip would be to get in contact with her P.I. and see how the investigation was going.

"Ava, please get Michael on the telephone for me please," she told her secretary.

Less than two minutes, she heard a knock on her office door, it was Shawn. Katrina, had no idea why he was here, but she was happy he had come to see her. She needed to ask him questions about Simone.

"Ava, please hold my calls and tell Michael I would like for him to come to the office around two this afternoon. Thanks." She releases the intercom button and turned her attention to Shawn.

"I just came to apologize for Simone's actions when you were in my office earlier," he said apologetically.

"No need for you to apologize. I am happy you came, I need to know any and every thing you can tell me about your secretary. There are some discrepancies in the information we have on file for her." At this point Katrina, folds her fingers and lean back in her chair to listen.

"Well I know what's on her file, but hmmm there seems to be way more to her than is there on that file. She always turns up wherever I go and I feel awkward around her. But I never say anything because she does exceptional work and it is always above par. Another thing is, I have been finding some weird things in my office since she started working for me, like a voodoo doll, locks of her hair, jars and sachets of bones." He sat with a puzzled look on his face as he spoke. All of what he was saying Katrina, took in and was in deep thought when her telephone rang. It was Ava, informing her that Michael would be at her office within the hour.

As she turned her attention back to Shawn, she realizes something very odd about his story, the items that were left around his office were somehow connected to voodoo rituals. But, she never said it to him.

"Thanks, Shawn, you have been most helpful," was her only response to his story.

Katrina, stood as she escorted him to the door. She needed time to clear her head and think before Michael got there. As he started to leave, he stopped so abruptly, that she bumped into him. For that brief second none of them spoke, but just enjoyed the brief physically closeness.

"Sorry, I just remembered something else. There was this one time, that I had me working on that merger deal with Cassie, from accounts. And for some strange reason, every time we met at my office, Simone kept interrupting and the last time Cassie, came by my office, Simone, threw some kind of liquid on her. She was out sick for months after that. Doctors never found out what was wrong with her, Cassie, now avoids me at all cost." He stood telling this story with this expression on his face that was more than just puzzlement and awe. Then Shawn, turned and told her that he had emailed her travel information to her office email address.

    He turned and left her office. Katrina, stood in shock and disbelief at what she heard, it was hard enough having to protect her mate from herself. Now it seems, she has to protect him from a witch.

4

    She barely had time to compose herself and process all the information she had receive when Michael, showed up. Katrina, was always happy to see him, for he was the only one who knew her secret, for he himself was a lycan and the only person she trusted. They had seen many great and terrible years together. She had known, Michael, from she was turned. Tristram Alexander, the head councilman for the lycan council, had assign Michael, to be her trainer and guardian during those crucial first years.

    But, we are getting ahead of ourselves, back to the matter at hand, the witch and where she came from was crucial. Especially now that Katrina, had found her alpha.

    Michael, as always greeted her with a hard but brief hug. Stood back and took her all in, he was proud of her accomplishments and even more proud that she had been the one turned. He had always seen her as the little sister he was robbed of when he was turned. Plus, he had trained her well, he had taught her not to hunt humans and used her powers very wiser, whether in her business or personal aspects of her life. She had proven to be a very great student and now she could not live without his guidance and advice.

    He knew what the call had meant, and, he had found out more than what he had bargain for. If he had been a mere mortal man, he would have been killed during this investigation. For once in his life, Michael, was in fear of losing his life during this investigation. He had lived for more than two hundred years and, in all that time he had never encountered witches and voodoo priestesses. Most of his adult life he had heard about them but never met or came across any.

He sat down on the couch in Katrina's office, his usual spot to pass on information or just for a visit to check on her. She sat next to him and allowed him time to gather whatever he needed to, to talk.

"Wow, where should I begin," Michael stated with a grim look in his eyes. "Well for starters, she is about ninety-seven years old, was an active and practice witch, with a coven that was dismantled most recently due to the death of their Umbra Supreme. Some say she is the one who killed her for revenge and power. She has been on the move for more than five years in search of her alpha warlock, which has brought her here to your company and Mr. Kenny." While his expression is serious, it is also painful, because he knows what he is about to tell Katrina, about her alpha mate, may crush her. "Katrina, what I am about to tell you may hurt and I have protected you all your life as a lycan, you are more to me than just a student, you have replaced my sister whom, I lost many years ago. Simone, is here because she has been in search of someone with Shawn's powers to over throw the witchcraft and voodoo world. She craves power and he is the key she needs to be the Umbra Supreme."

Katrina, sits and absorbs all that she is being told. But, for some reason she feels and knows Michael has more information for her. So, she sits and waits, as he takes out a manila folder and passes it to her. Katrina opens it and just stares at the photos in it. Examining each one closer. Each photo is just as or more graphic than the other. All of scenes apparently from the murder of the Supreme within the coven's walls. One shows a woman in her mid to late thirties, completely naked and spread out on the floor in some archaic pose. Her eyes were gorged out, her mouth cut into a joker's grin, her throat was slit in some morbid way, her heart had been torn out, cut open and pushed into her eyes, ears and mouth, her legs are spread apart and she had been gutted like a fish, with her internal organs placed all around her. Katrina, saw that there is something written on the wall in her blood but, she can't understand the language. She realizes how much danger Shawn is in where Simone is concerned. She will have to act and quickly.

Michael watches all the expressions that pass across Katrina's face, and he knows that there is cause for serious concern. He always wants to protect for all the evils in this world, but he knows he can't. All he can do is just to be there whenever she needs him.

"So what is our next move?" he asks. He gives her time to think and gather herself.

She turns and smiles saying, "I will protect what is mine at all cost! Find out as much as you can about how to destroy her. Simone will have to be killed in order to save Shawn."

Michael, is not surprised at her response, after all it is what he expected from her. Cold and calculated as she does business is also her approach to her personal life. He will support her decision, plus he likes all the excitement investigating brings in his life.

He gets up and prepares to leave, but as an afterthought, "So how will we proceed in the total protection of Shawn?"

She really hadn't thought about that as yet, but she had some ideas on how she would. Katrina, knew she had the full support of the council where Shawn was concerned. So her first move would be to meet with Tristram and ask him to call a meeting of the council for her.

"Michael, do you know if Tristram has returned from his trip to the council in Italy?" was her question and first move.

"I am not sure, but I will check and let you know by the end of the day." He hugged her and lightly kissed her on both cheeks.

Alone once again, Katrina sits and think about how she can protect Shawn without him knowing. She has to rethink how she will tell him that there is a battle raging for him and his power. With this in mind, she forgot to ask Michael, what power does Shawn have. All of this is running through her mind as she picks up her phone to call home and let Claudette know that they will be having a guest for dinner tonight.

"Hey girlfriend, how are things going? Just called to let you know that I have invited someone over for dinner tonight." She waited on eggshells for her long time housekeeper and friend to answer.

Claudette couldn't believe her ears, Katrina, bringing a guest over for dinner. Mmm wonder what this is all about, she has never invited anyone over before.

"Ok and yes no problem. Do you want me to fix anything special for dinner?" she asks as she stands with this bewildered look on her face.

"You know what just surprise us. Expect us any time after seven this evening. Thanks hun and now you see why I love you so? See you when I get home." Katrina hung up and now picked up her phone to call

Shawn and invite him over for dinner, but what excuse could she use to get him to come home with her.

"Hi, again. I was wondering if you had any plans for tonight?"

Shawn, recognizes the extension right away, and his palms start sweating, heart skips a few beats before he answers the line. With a smile on his lips, he waits as she asks her question. He wants to make her sweat and wait but he can't.

"I am free tonight. What do you have in mind?" he says, still grinning like a school boy talking to his crush.

"Well a private dinner for two, say my place. You can catch a ride with me when I leave for the evening." She waits on a response with her breath held.

His response is breathtakingly slow for her and fast for him.

"Yes of that would be great."

He can't believe that, the woman he has lusted after, yearned for, for almost three years, has just invited him to a dinner for two at her home. He couldn't believe how his day was turning out. It was getting better by the second not even minute. Not even Simone's bad actions earlier could not dampen his mood.

Simone, glanced in Shawn's office, she had a clear view, because he left the door open. She was none to please to see him grinning and whispering on the telephone. She had known from it rang that it was, Katrina. It made her blood boiled knowing that out of all the attractive men in the office, Katrina, had chosen hers to mess with. Simone, knew she would have a fight on her hands to get him, and with Katrina in the mix it made things even more complicated.

She watched him pack up his files and pick up his briefcase as if he was ready to leave for the day, but then she remembered he had a business lunch with one of his clients. Simone had no idea that he had a dinner date with Katrina later that night.

He returned to the office after three that afternoon, and told Simone to hold all his calls because he had to go over the contracts that their new client had just signed. She complied as any great secretary would, so that her boss would be happy. She heard him humming under his breath, which was something new. About three hours later, she poked her heard in Shawn's office to let him know she was leaving for the day. She found him singing and grinning like a fool.

"You are sure in a great mood this evening," she smiled.

"I should be, we just signed a multibillion dollar contract with a new client. Everything went better today than I imagined they would." He was excited more about his date with Katrina rather than any damned contract, no matter how much money was involved.

"Great to see you finally smiling. You want to celebrate over a drink?" she asked excitedly.

"Maybe some other time. I have made other plans for today," was his response.

"Ok no problem. Rain check then?"

"Sure."

Simone was not disappointed as she walked away, she was furious. She said her goodnights and walked down to the underground garage, and waited for him to leave so that she could follow him. She had a bit of a wait but he emerged shortly after six, followed by none other than Ms. Hannah herself. Now she really was furious.

She watched has Katrina's private car pulled up and Shawn held the door open for her to go in. Simone, made a vow to get even with the bitch at all cost.

The car pulled out of the garage with Simone following behind with murder in her heart and blood in her eyes. The idea of that bitch taking her opportunity to become the ultimate Umbra Supreme.

5

The minute she came out of the elevator, Katrina, saw Simone sitting in her car. Across the parking lot. She didn't know whether to be angry or concerned for Shawn's safety. But she knew one thing for certain that she really had to protect him at all cost.

Katrina, knowing that Simone would follow them, told her driver to make a quick stop at Michael's office a few blocks away. She then makes a quick telephone call to Michael, letting him know she is on her way there with Shawn.

"Ok, that's great because I have some news for you, and I get to meet your alpha," is Mike's quick response, with that Katrina hung up her telephone.

Shawn, at this point is not quite comfortable and he doesn't fully know why, but he knows it's not Katrina that is making him uncomfortable. But, what or who could be the cause of his discomfort?

He tries to relax as Katrina offers him a drink from the mini bar in the car. He refuses simply because he doesn't drink any alcoholic beverages. Wow, yet another trait that Katrina admires and find endearing.

For her, a sober man is a clear headed one. Plus, it is best that her alpha not be a drinker, due to the tasks ahead of them both as the next ruling couple of her pack.

Only recently has she found out that she is next in line to rule her pack, but she needs a strong alpha to rule with her. Tristram, had already found her alpha, but as usual she was reluctant in getting close to him. But, when she laid eyes on Shawn, she knew she had to have him, not knowing at the time that he was designed to be her alpha. Now that she knew he was hers, she would protect from every threat possible until he was able to protect himself.

While he was sipping on his drink, Shawn, kept a steady eye on Katrina. He watched her body go from relaxed to tensed in a second, not knowing why and afraid to ask. He just sat and watched as familiar buildings passed the car's window in silence.

Ten minutes later, Katrina got out the car and entered the high rise that was Michael's P.I. firm. Walking with the confidence and esteem of a woman on a great mission, she went straight up to his office on the twenty-second floor. As she entered the entrance to his office, his secretary greeted her and let her go straight in.

Michael, was seated behind a massive desk almost cover completely in photos and files. As she got closer, most of the photos on his desks were of Simone or Shawn. In each photo of Shawn, you could see Simone in the background following him. Scary as it was, it infuriated Katrina to know to what extremes this woman would go to get Shawn.

Michael got up and led Katrina to the chairs in front of his desk to be seated.

"I was about to call when you called me. I found out more information that I need to pass on to you. Have a seat so I can get started. I noticed you were looking at the photos and yes she follows him just about any and everywhere." Michael sat back down behind his desk.

Michael, starts by telling Katrina, how Simone not only follows Shawn, but how she has him down to a science. She knows when he gets up. When he sleeps, she has even gone so far has to sleep in his bed when he made business trips. She is proving to be a real psycho as far as Michael and his investigating team was concerned.

Simone, is proving that she will have to be eliminated at any cost. She can become a threat to Katrina's pack, and as future leader of it, she has to inform the council and ask their advice on what they will allow her to do.

"Thanks, Mike. Please keep me informed of any new developments. Oh, did you hear from Tristram?" At this point she really needs his advice.

"Yes, I did and he should be contacting you some time tonight."

Katrina gets up and leaves Mike's office with answers, but yet more questions. But, she knows her next moves. First, contact the P.I. Jerome McPhee, then talk to Tristram.

She returns to the car and heads home. Katrina makes small talk with Shawn, because she realizes that he is no longer comfortable. She must do all she can to help him out of the dilemma that he doesn't know he is in.

Shawn, leans closer to Katrina, just to inhale her scent. He is intoxicated by her, but he feels he would hurt her if she ever found out about his night adventures to her home, especially in her bedroom. He realizes that he is in love with her, and must make his own and soon. He fears that she will not want him after she finds out his secret. Shawn, has to make her understand that it was never his intention to fall in love with her, but that it just seemed to happen.

Katrina, notices that Shawn, is trying to get closer to her and she relaxes so that he can lean closer. He has a musky, masculine scent, that is a pheromone for her, she is finding it hard not to touch him. She can hear his heart speed up and his breathing deepens as he inhales her scent.

Her cell phone rings and she knows that it's Jerome, she had forgotten to tell Mike, that he can pass on the information on Simone to him. She makes a quick mental note to call Mike as soon as she is done talking to Jerome.

"Goodnight, Mr. McPhee. I do have some information for you but unfortunately I can't meet with you until tomorrow evening. I will let Michael Ambrose, my P.I., give you all that he has found out about Simone." she informs him.

Jerome, is slightly disappointed, because he was looking forward to having a private evening with her. But, business has to come first, plus, he knows that she is with him. He has to compose himself before he answers her.

"Thank you for all your help, Ms. Hannah. I look forward to seeing you tomorrow night." he sighs knowing he may never have her.

Katrina, smiles to herself, because she felt the disappointment and jealousy coming through the phone from Jerome. She hangs up, leans back and enjoy the ride home with her soon to be alpha. Even though she knows, the psycho bitch Simone, is following them.

Shawn tries to read her but can't. But he senses danger nearby, and he will soon have to face reality and let Katrina know the whole truth about himself.

6

He couldn't believe his eyes; how could she be living in this massive estate alone. Katrina, just smiled at the awe she saw on Shawn's face when the driver turned into her driveway. She was elated to see him finally relaxing.

As she got out the car, her driver asked if she would be needing him later that evening, she was about to say no but thought it wiser to tell him that he would have to take Shawn home. She saw the disappointment on Shawn's face but paid it no mind. She had her plans for the evening and sticking with them. Furthermore, his safety was priority now to her.

Claudette, greeted them at the front door. She led Shawn to the living room area, while Katrina went to freshen up.

"I hope that I am not being nosey, but how long have you worked for Katrina?" he asked Claudette, politely.

Her response she knew would shock and amaze him. "For more than twenty years now."

He looked at her in disbelief, but he knew she was telling him the truth. Shawn, wondered how this could be possible when Katrina, had to be in her early to mid-thirties. She had to be no more than thirty-five, thirty-six the most. Claudette looked like she herself was no more than forty. But, he knew from his instincts that he was not being lied to.

He sat quietly down in one of the most beautiful rooms he had ever seen. It had a huge fireplace, very comfy styles dual couches all in one tropical color or another. There was a portrait of Katrina, over the fireplace, but it couldn't be her. The woman in the portrait was dressed like a lady from the late eighteen hundreds.

Shawn, sat in deep thought over the portrait, when Claudette came in to ask him if he wanted a drink while he waited.

"The lady in the portrait, is she some family to Katrina?"

"No, that is Katrina. She had this crazy idea to have it done dressed in that attire." Claudette said with a polite smile. This time he knew he was being lied to, but about what he wasn't sure.

Claudette, went over to the bar and got him a soda on ice, because she already knew he wasn't a drinker. She took it to him and left him alone once again in the living room. Claudette, then told him that dinner will be served in an hour.

Shortly after, Katrina, entered the living room wearing a casual pair of slacks with a turtle neck sweater. She sat down next to him, and he immediately became all too aware of her nearness.

"I see Claudette, has been entertaining you while I was getting dressed." Her smile was incredible and breathtaking.

"Hmm...yes she did." he said with a sigh.

Her smile was even sweeter as she turned to face him. She was figuring out how she was going to tell him all that she needed to without him freaking out. So, she decided to start with the photos that she had gotten from Michael, then she would tell him all that she had learn so far about Simone and then she would show Shawn her true self. Katrina, then got up and brought the manila folder from off the bar where Claudette had put it.

"I need you to brace yourself for what I about to tell and show you. There are things going on around you that I know you don't and can't understand. I will try my best to bring some clarification to some of it. I, myself am still coming to grips with what I have found out so far."

That being said she handed the folder to him and braced herself for his reaction. He sat with the folder on his lap not knowing if he wanted to open it, but he knew he needed to see what was inside.

With his breath held, he opened the folder and took each photo out and examined it, like it was some type of strange and dreadful creature. His expressions and body language was all over the map, from fright to shock to just plain horror. Shawn, wanted to ask so badly what these photos and the people in them had to do with him. He sat a minute longer just thinking what to say next, but he had no idea.

Katrina, realize this was all a major shock to him. She placed her hand gently on top of his. He jumped has if he had been hit by lightning. She looked at him as if to say, 'whatever you want and need to know I will tell you.'

"I know it is a lot to take in but, I felt you needed to know and that now was the best time to do it. All I have learned so far is that Simone seeks to claim you as her mate and that she is a witch with deadly intentions. So far as I know, she has only committed one murder and that is the lady you see in the photos." She moved closer to him as a form and source of comfort.

"How is this even possible? There are no such things as witches!" was all he could stomach to say.

Katrina, felt his confusion and didn't really know how she was going to help him through this. She knew she had to find a way, because he would have to protect himself the best way he could.

Shawn turned to Katrina with questioning eyes. "How and when did you get this information?"

"Today from a PI named Jerome McPhee and Michael my companies PI. It was a double whammy type of day for me too, so you are not only trying to absorb all of this."

Just then Claudette came in to let them know dinner was ready.

Katrina led Shawn to an intimately set dining room. Candles were lit everywhere. He looks around taking in the scenery forgetting what he has just seen and began to focus solely on Katrina. He had all intentions no matter what they talked about and discussed to make love to her tonight.

Reading his mind, Katrina leaned close to him and whispered, "That won't happen unless I let you take me. But my plan is to take you." She smiled wickedly and took her seat.

7

Over dinner they spoke quietly about how he would have to act when he returned to the office the next day. He had to remain as neutral and compose as possible, so as not to let Simone know that she had been found out.

They also finalized their travel arrangements for their trip that weekend. Katrina, told him that no matter what they had to keep doing what they would normally do. They had to give to signals that they knew what she had planned, but Katrina still had more for Shawn to know.

After dinner she led him to the terrace off from her living room. As she sipped on a glass of her favorite chardonnay, she leaned against the railing. Shawn, just looked at her loving what he saw, the pure beauty of her. The way her brown hair fell to her shoulders, he had never seen her with her hair down until now and it made her even more beautiful and sensual.

Katrina, knew she was being watched and she was enjoying basking in the eyes of her soon to be mate. She allowed him to believe he was the seducer, when all along she was seducing him. She turned to let her hair fall back over the railing as she looked up at the moon. A war was raging in her, whether to show him now or to wait until after they had made love. She thought it best to show her wolfen side now before she could convince herself out of it.

"Shawn, I am about to show you something, there will be no need to be afraid. I just need you to stay calm and know that I will never hurt you in any way." She stepped toward him, held his face in both of her soft hands and kissed him for the first time.

He was taken aback when she kissed him. It started off slow, soft and sweet. Almost like that of an innocent school girl having a first kiss. It got hotter, and more passionate as she bit down gently on his lower lip, her hands began gently pulling his hair. As the kiss got more sensual and passionate as their tongues explored each other's' mouths, their hands were also exploring their bodies. Katrina, broke the kiss so abruptly that Shawn nearly lost his balance. One thing at a time she thought and it was her time to show her true animalistic self.

She turned her back to him as she felt the heat surge through her body. Her clothes seem to melt away from the heat that permeated from her. This would be a slow painful process for her tonight, because she had to let him see the full transformation. The cry that came from her lips was a measure of human and animal, as her skin began to tear and bones began their process of elongating and stretching. Katrina's body hair began to grow longer, her fingers and hands stretch gruesome and painfully long and were transformed into paws along with her legs toes and feet. Her beautiful face, was stretched bones were heard cracking, breaking and relocating during this excruciatingly painful transformation. When it was all over before Shawn, stood the most beautiful silver wolf, that was bigger than any wolf he had seen in his life.

Katrina, walked over to Shawn, as if she was his pet and stood before. He started to back away and the wall stopped him. He didn't know whether to run, or to pet her, but he knew for certain she would not hurt him. Not even in this form. He mustered up the courage and walked to her and hugged her, like she had never known. She started the transformation back to her human form. By the time he let her go she was fully human and naked before him. He took off his shirt and wrapped her in it, even though the sight of her naked was more beautiful as a human than a wolf. He wanted to bask in her beauty, but he had to be a gentleman and give her some privacy, especially now that she had revealed herself to him. Now he knew he had to be with her, because now he understood his dreams.

Even as a child, Shawn, knew he was different from everybody else. He had the ability to do things that no one else around him could. The first time he knew he was different, was in the second grade, when the bully in his class threatened to take his lunch and lunch money. He felt himself lift out his body and watched from a distance as the bully tried to hit him an d kept missing. The second time he remembered it happening was when he was seventeen and had a mad crush on a girl in this class. For some reason every night he fell asleep he had dreamt that he was sleeping in her bed next to her. Until one day she approached him and asked why he kept creeping in her room at night, naked.

He found, as he got older, that he could see into the hearts and thoughts of others. Not only could he read their minds, he also how the power of persuasion, to make them change their minds to do what he wanted them to do. Weird thing was he never used this power to harm anyone, but to help out those that were in danger of being hurt by others.

As he sat holding her, he realized that there was more going on between them than he even knew. All those nights of waking up in a cold sweat from dreams he could remember and from those he wished he could forget. Those nights of dreaming of running from something horrible and terrifying with a woman he had yet to meet. Those nights of wet dreams of a woman more sexual and sensual than any he had ever been with. Those nights of waking up scared of losing someone he thought he would never meet. And, now here she was in his arms, looking at him through eyes that had seen years of broken and loneliness. Here she was waiting to be held, to be kissed, to be caressed, to be made love to and to be loved. All his life he had searched for answers to the unanswerable questions in his head, and now they were finally being answered.

The woman in his dreams had been Katrina. Now as to whom or what they were running from had yet to be discovered in reality, but he knew that she was his and he would eternally be hers.

Katrina, loved the way he smelled and even more the way he was holding her. Like a man protecting his most prized and treasured possession. She fell more into his embrace and he held on even tighter to her. She knew that he was definitely her alpha and after tonight they would have want of no others in their lives.

She turned her face up toward his with a questioning look in her eyes. He answered those eyes by place a soft kiss on each eyelid. Then he kissed her nose, her cheeks and then he invaded her mouth with such passion unknown to him. He had to possess her and make her his own.

Without a word he lifted her and carried her to the nearest couch in the living room. Their passion was an unbridled one. He spoke no words, just bit, kissed, nibbled and caressed every exposed inch of her. She. On the other hand, started shredding his clothes, fighting to feel his flesh against hers. The heat builds between them till it's as if they are going to explode.

Shawn, just about exploded as he felt Katrina's hands fumbling with the zipper on his pants. He gasped for air as she found him hard and throbbing. He could contain himself no longer, he had to be in her and now!

He pressed her into the couch with the weight of his body. Kissing her as his hands travelled down her body to find her lips wet and blossoming as a flower in spring. Pushing his two of his finger inside of her, as she arched her hips to meet them. There was no want of waiting for both of them.

"Please, I need you in me now!" she whispered in a husky voice no longer hiding her desire to mate with him, and only him.

Shawn, complied as he straightened to take her to be completely his for life. He pushed so hard to be inside her till he thought he had hurt her, but she smiled looking up at him. Because, she like a little pain with her pleasure. He felt her lips and then her walls squeezing him as he went deeper inside of her. He couldn't believe the fire the burned inside her. It was so hot, wet and throbbing inside of her till he was around on the verge of a massive orgasm, but he fought to hold back so that she too could enjoy him, as he was enjoying her. She pulled him closer to her, till he could feel the sweat running down her stomach. Her back arched as he plunged deeper into her with every pounding stroke.

"All I need to know now is. Are you sure that this is what you truly want?" she asked between strokes and breaths.

"Yes. You are mine for life, as I will be yours," was his reply.

That was all Katrina needed to hear, her transformation was quick, from woman to wolf, as she bit down into his shoulder has they both climaxed. It was blindly explosion of extreme pain and pleasure for Shawn, but he knew that this was what was meant to be, but most importantly this is what he wanted. To be hers for an eternity.

From the moment Simone heard that howl she knew that Katrina had mated with Shawn. But, not all hope was lost, because she had another way of getting him to be hers.

8

Even though Simone, was a bit disappointed, she still had an ace up her sleeve. 'Boy, wait till Katrina saw what she had in store for her.' She will fight to the death if she has to in order to get Shawn and the Umbra Supreme's power. She would invite her ally to the office tomorrow just to see the look on Katrina's face.

Still park in front of the driveway that led to Katrina's home, Simone pulled out her cellphone and made a call to Keven Mathieu. Kevin was a pivotal piece in her scheme to destroy Katrina and get Shawn as her prized possession.

"Kevin, darling, sorry to just be returning your call, slight change in plans. I will be more than delighted to come and see you tonight. I should be at your hotel in an hour," she purred into the phone with an evil grin across her lips.

Simone hung up with her plan around in motion, started up her Jag and pulled off. She already knew how to manipulate Kevin into doing her bidding. He was the ultimate ally in this scenario, because he was the lycan who turned Katrina. Simone knew he still a torch in his heart for Katrina, and this is how she was going to use him to not only get Shawn, but ultimate power as the Supreme of the most powerful coven, the witchcraft world would ever know.

As she pulls up in front of Kevin's hotel, she knows that she will have to reassure him that her plan will work. The question is how will she do this. She knows he would never sleep with her, because his heart and body belongs, as far as he is concerned, to no one else but Katrina.

Simone goes up to the penthouse and rang the doorbell. Kevin appeared almost instantly after she rang. He was naked except for a towel, which he had wrapped around himself. He had the built of a god. A chiseled chest, abs that any woman would want and yearn to feel against her own, a strong jaw line with a cleft chin, with a smile that would melt an ice queen's heart.

"Oh I wasn't expecting you so soon, Simone. Come in please make yourself comfortable while I get dressed," he said as he turned and headed for the bedroom.

Simone, couldn't help but admire the ass that he may have taken years to develop and maintain, or was it just a lycan gene. She couldn't help but to follow him into the bedroom. It had been years since she had felt the touch of a man, too many years in fact to count.

Kevin knew she had followed him into the bedroom, he would give her more than she had bargained for with him. He turned to face her and dropped his towel. She stopped sudden at the shocked at the sheer size of him, she guessed it was the lycan gene. 'Mmm.... thank goodness for those genes.'

"Can I help you with something, Simone?" he looked at her with lust in his eyes. He hadn't touched a woman in close to a century and he needed to have a release and now was as good a time as any.

Before she had chance to respond, he was on her, ripping her clothes and biting her neck. She was thrown on the king size bed with such force that she almost bounced off of it. He was on her, yet again, before she had a chance to recover, his roughness was appealing to her, as she was tossed flat on her back. He entered her with one swift movement it made the room spin. His strokes were hard, pounding and merciless.

"I am going to do to you what no man has ever thought of doing to you," he growled next to her ear.

She melted as he spoke these words. He pulled out of her, nibbling, licking and sucking his way down to where her thighs met in a hot, steamy junction. His mouth was ravenously exploring her wet pussy and she couldn't help but to moan with an unbridled passion. Simone had never experienced anything like this before and she was loving it.

Kevin became harder hearing her moans of lust and passion. He pushed two finger in her wet pussy as his tongue took trips around the world on her clit. He couldn't hold out any longer he had to be in her again, and now!

He turned her over on her stomach, raised her ass, and slammed in her from behind. His strokes were so powerful, that she was crying out not in pain but pleasure. Begging him to fuck her even harder and faster. With every stroke he pushed his fingers in her ass. She wanted to pull away but couldn't, he had a tight grip with his free hand on her waist. He pulled out of her hot, wet, sucking pussy and slowly inch by painful inch he went deeper in her ass. She cried out in pain but he didn't care, he was enjoying her cries. He was getting harder and more aroused with every scream that came out of her mouth. The looser her ass became the harder he slammed into her. Just as he was about to climaxed, he heard her screams turn to moans of pleasure. Their climax was hot and intense. He pulled out and collapsed on the bed next to her.

"So what are your plans for my beloved, Katrina?"

Simone was surprised at how fast he could shift from hot sex straight into business. But, she didn't mind the swift change, it got her mind back in the game of destroying Katrina.

"Perish the thought of killing my Katrina, else I will end you and now. Trust me, you don't want to cross me," he looked at her with hate in his eyes.

Simone, recoiled from his harsh words, as he reached to squeeze her bare breast. He was rough with his squeezing and pinching of her nipple. Even though it was extremely painful, Simone was getting aroused by it.

Kevin, knew what he was doing to her and abruptly stopped, leaving her yearning for his touch. He had plans to inflict more pain to her but not now, that have to wait until later. They had business to discuss and plans to make.

9

She woke up sore but sexually satisfied. Katrina could hear his deep breathing next to her, she relaxed knowing he was safe with her. Katrina, knew that they would face a battle from Simone, but what type she didn't know. She would now have to meet with the pack council and get some advice.

She hated waking him, because he looked so peaceful sleeping, but it was time for them to head into the office. But, before she would leave the house, she would contact Tristram, and ask him to convene the council.

Katrina, awoke Shawn, and allowed him to get ready first to leave. He looked at her, as if to say what he was going to wear, after all she had shredded his clothes the night before.

Smiling sheepishly, she said, "Look in the closet on the left. I am sure you can find something suitable to wear to the office."

She had been shopping for months for him without his knowledge. Shawn, looked in the closet and was shocked and pleasantly surprised at the wardrobe of attire that was in there. All of his favorite styles and colors were in there. He turned looked at her and just smiled. A smile that lit up his whole body, seeing that he was naked. She loved looking at him. He was a beautiful sight to behold and what he had naturally would be enhanced with time and his new lycan genes.

Katrina, knew she needed to get a start on her day, even though she enjoyed admiring her mate more. She let him google over his new wardroom as she prepared to make her call to Tristram.

"Good morning, Alexanders residence." It was their housekeeper, Mrs. Malcolm.

"Hi, Mrs. M., this Katrina, can I speak to Tristram please?"

She told Katrina, to wait a minute. Less than a minute later he was on the line. He was elated to hear from her.

"Even though I know the grim circumstances for your call, I am still happy to hear from you. It has been too long, Katrina," Tristram said.

She knew she had been distancing herself from a man that was not only the most powerful lycan, but a man who was a real father to her. Katrina really hated how things had turned out between them over the past few years. But, she had to do what she thought was best for her. Her company was just starting to make her name for itself and things were looking great, she didn't want a mate and the responsibility of the council. She wanted to be carefree and footloose with nothing to tie her down.

Now, looking back she felt some regret for having disappointed, Tristram. Katrina, had to push pass the past and mend her relationship with him and fast. If she ever needed him and the council, it was now!

Katrina brought him up to speed on what all was going on. He smiled knowing she hadn't told him he was right about her alpha and that they had already mated. Nonetheless, he knew a pack meeting with the council was more than needed.

"Tonight at my home, say around eight o'clock, we will have the meeting. Let Michael know. Also, I heard that Kevin Mathieu is back in town." Tristram, knew that this was not only news to her but a shock.

Katrina didn't know how to respond to his last statement, so she sat in silence.

'So, Kevin was back. Wonder what has brought him back.' She was thinking, as she vaguely heard Tristram say his goodbye and hung up.

She sat there thinking about the last encounter she had with Kevin, it was a mixture of hate, pain, anger and love she had, and will always feel for him. After all he had been the lycan who had turned her over a century ago. Kevin, was then and still is an arrogant son of a bitch, who knew which buttons to push and pull in her. For as much has she loved him, he would do something to make her hate him, so they had a love hate type of relationship.

What distracted her from these thoughts of Kevin, was hearing the shower turn off. Then she remembered her first of many nights to come with her mate. She knew now that Tristram had been right about Shawn. He truly was made just for her, her ultimate alpha. For a guy his age, Shawn, was wise beyond his years and a great advisor, both qualities she had always searched for but never found until now.

She had wanted to catch him in the shower, to make love before they would leave for the office, but no such luck. So she headed to the bathroom to shower and get ready for her day ahead. He stopped her just as she stepped in the bathroom. Lifted her up and placed her on the countertop between the face bowls. He was hard as she felt him spread her legs to enter her.

"What took you so long? I couldn't wait all morning in the shower you know," he whispers in her ear as he entered her.

She was wet and hot just from the idea of him being hers. It didn't take long for them both to climax. He held her in place as his harden cock stayed firmly planted in her as he ejaculated more than usual inside of her heat.

"Now, we both need to shower," she growled as she broke away from him and headed to the shower.

They got dressed quickly after another hot round in the shower and headed down to breakfast. Claudette, had prepared steak, medium rare, and onions, along with toast, eggs and coffee for their breakfast. Shawn immediately asked for milk and orange juice, preferring them over the coffee offered.

Shortly after the car arrived to carry them to the office, where Katrina knew that Simone would be waiting in the garage to see if they would return together this morning. She would be sadly disappointed though, because Katrina had her driver pick up Shawn's car from the office the night before and bring it to the house this morning.

Shawn arrived and hour before she did. Katrina made a few stops before she headed into the office. As her driver pulled up to the offices' entrance she felt rather than saw, Simone's glare from the elevators in the lobby.

Katrina, stopped at the security desk inquiring about any strange visitors to the office that morning. The officer informed her about a Mr. Kevin Mathieu, who had demanded to see her and only her. She asked if they had allowed him access, and was told that her secretary had vouched for him.

"I hope that's not a problem, Ms. Hannah," the officer inquired.

"No. he is a very old friend and is always demanding," she smiled and walked to the elevators.

When she got to her office her secretary a timid woman got up to warn her about Kevin's foul mood.

"Ava, haven't you learned anything from working with me all these years. Don't worry I know just how to handle him," she smiled warmly at Ava and went in her office.

10

"Kevin, darling how are you? I haven't seen you in slow long," Katrina cooed as she stepped in her office.

He just about melted at her words. If it was one woman he had desired to bed and make love to, it was always, Katrina. But he knew it was not meant to be. His love for her would never be made known to anyone, not even, Katrina.

He sat comfortably behind her desk and look as if he belonged there. In all the years she had known him, that she finally could resist him. From he had first turned her, she wanted to bed him, but he would turn her on and leave her hanging.

This time around there would be no turning on, no leaving her hanging and now that she had found her mate she was completely happy. She took a deep breath and stepped further into her office. The look she gave him was ice cold and devastating to his heart. Katrina, had found her mate and had already mated with him. Kevin, knew now that he was no longer going to have any hold over her.

Kevin, could smell him on her, even though she had showered. He arose and walk toward her, bent down and smelled between her legs. He looked up and with a wicked smile on his lips, winked.

"So my fair, Katrina, is no longer mine to have. I see you have finally mated and I am very jealous that it wasn't me," he said with wicked intentions.

She smiled as she took her seat behind her desk. Katrina, knew that Kevin meant every word he said. He truly was jealous of not being her mate. He had wanted her from the day he turned almost one hundred and twenty-five years ago. Kevin had always known there was something special about Katrina, until recently he didn't know what. But, he was not here on a casual visit, he was here to meet her mate and destroy him, to reclaim his fair Katrina.

It was amazing to see how far she had come and how much she had accomplished from the last time he made contact with her. Normally, Kevin, would always observe her from a distance. It was easier to hide his pain of having never claimed her as his own. Though he was an old lycan he was smitten with Katrina, from the day he saw her in her native village. He had gone so far as to ask her father for her hand in marriage, but was offered that of her sister. While yes, Katherine, was a beautiful woman, Katrina, on the other hand was strong, independent and beautiful, the qualities he had been looking for in a mate. Most women he had come across in her era was only good for one thing, and her sister was no exception to that rule. But, his fair Katrina, would never let him touch her and he love her even more for being so.

The night that he had turned his fair Katrina, was a night he will never forget. He had just taken her sister. Kevin, had done things to Katherine that were unheard of in those days. He practically raped and she enjoyed it. She gave in without any form of a fight. He had been extremely rough with her, because he couldn't have his fair Katrina, he had her bent over a gravestone and rammed into her without mercy. Kevin went so far has to fuck her in the ass without preparing or warning her. His anger was more than he could bear. 'How dear her father says whom he could and couldn't wed!'

He would have her as his own, and before the night was out. After he was done with Katherine, he tossed her to the side like a discarded old rag. Kevin went off in a rage, even is transformation that night wasn't painful. He had her scent in his nostrils and before he knew it he was on her. To claim, to possess, to have for all eternity and there was no one to stop him.

Katrina thought she had heard something following her, but was not sure if it human. She wanted to turn and run, but the fighter in her told her to stand her ground and that she did. When she turned around and came face to face with a huge and yet beautiful wolf. She had seen them before in the woods, but none so majestic and beautiful as this one. It was silver streaked with black, with eyes that seemed almost human. Those eyes her every move, as if calculating what to do next. The wolf just casually walked up to her, as a lover would have done. Even though it was four times the size of a regular wolf, Katrina, felt no need to be afraid of it. She was mesmerized by it and its beauty. Then it leapt in the air and on her, it was so sudden that she didn't feel its fangs cutting into her flesh. She fainted when she heard it speak.

"You will forever be mine and mine alone."

Sitting in the chair opposite his fair Katrina, Kevin reminiscences of their first real encounter. His grins with all the thoughts of what could have been and what will be, when it comes to his, fair Katrina.

"I missed you and needed to see you," he said in his baritone voice, that would usually send sparks and ripples up her spine, for once it had no effect on her.

"Oh really. Mmm... you missed me. What did I ever do to deserve such attention?" she asked unbelievingly. "So, Kevin, why are you really here?"

He laughed in such a way that it made her angry. Kevin, was here for more than he would ever let her know. He had an invested interest in Katrina, and would do all within his power to forever protect, even from himself.

"Tristram, called me because he had concerns about your safety and the safety of your mate, Shawn. Plus, I was in town any way," he sat with his legs crossed and his fingers forming a steeple in front of his lips.

"Although, as we both know, you are more than capable to protect yourself as well as your mate. I wonder, my fair Katrina, have you told him who and what you are? And, how well did he take the news? Mmm... my darling."

Just he thought of him knowing about Shawn, crawled Katrina's flesh. She had known from the first time she had laid eyes on Kevin, that he would stop at nothing to make her his. Sadly, for him fate had other plans.

"Oh I see and you just decided to come and see me," she said.

"Actually, I am in town on some serious business, that may be of some concern of yours. I am interested in buying a company and need your expertise on what I should be considering. You know the pros and cons, that type of thing."

Katrina, knew when he was serious and when she was being played, but with Kevin, business was business and he never mixed the two. She relaxed and asked him to bring her up to date on the company he was buying and its purchase cost, overhead and other expenses.

He filled her in on the details. He pulled a file folder out of his briefcase containing all the relevant information. Kevin, leaned over the desk to catch a glimpse of Katrina's cleavage, just as there was a knock on her door. Shawn stepped into the office as Kevin was kissing Katrina on the lips.

Kevin, grins wickedly at Katrina, turns and introduced himself to Shawn. He shakes his hand, thanks Katrina for her assistance in his new business venture and leaves.

Shawn, just stands looking from the door to Katrina.

11

Katrina, had already told Shawn about Kevin, and what he will try to do to make him jealous. Shawn, fully saw and now understood what she had meant.

"He sure is a piece of work," was he quirky response to what Kevin had tried. He knew, within himself, that no man, or woman for that matter would ever make him jealous of where he stood in Kat's life.

She laughed whole heartedly, relieved that Shawn was not the jealous type and secure in where he stood in her life. Katrina, was still laughing as Shawn, bent over to kiss her.

"So why was he here, Kat?" he asked with an air of concern.

She didn't know where to begin, but she told Shawn that Kevin initially came for the pack meeting. Also that he was investing in a new company and wanted her advice and expertise. But, deep down she had known Kevin was in town for more than he had mentioned.

Shawn, had a feeling that Katrina, wasn't telling him al she knew, but whatever it was, he would wait until she was ready. He had never felt this way for anyone before and he didn't want to ruin it. He had fallen in love with Katrina from day one and now knowing how she felt for him, he fell even deeper in love with her.

He made himself comfortable in the chair opposite hers. He had come to her office with the final preparations for their trip.

"We will be staying at a nice little bed and breakfast on the main island. There will be a boat to transport us, as needed between the island and the cay. Also, Mr. Knowles, has informed me that you will have a staff of three to assist you with whatever you may need done to the house, while you are there. But I was thinking that you may feel more comfortable carrying Claudette along," he smiled sheepishly, for he had also fallen in love with her housekeeper.

"Mmm... I see, Claudette, has won your heart as well," she smiled happily knowing that the man she loved, had fallen in love with the one woman, who had been a real mother to her.

"I have already made her arrangements to leave a day earlier, so that she got a better lay of the land, for when we would arrive," he said, thinking of the wild night they would have when Claudette had left.

"You sly little lycan, you. What would your mother say if she only knew about your wicked plans?" Katrina laughed wickedly.

She walked over to him, and kissed him at if it was her first time. Blushing like a school girl, she backed away as his hands started travelling up her skirt. Teasingly she ran her tongue over her lips.

Katrina, sure knew how to tease and seduce any man she wanted, and right now and forever, she only wanted Shawn. With her index finger she beckoned him over to the couch, that was against the back wall of her office, away from all the windows in seclusion.

"Wait, I just have to do one thing," she went to her desk and pressed the intercom, "Ava, please hold my calls for the next hour please."

Shawn, barely could contain his excitement and arousal. He had never had sex in any office before, and this was going to be an awesome experience, that they both would want to relive. Katrina, locked her office door and walked over to him.

But, Shawn had another idea, he wanted to try something he had always dreamed of doing but never had a willing partner. He was sure Katrina would be game and up for just about anything.

"Honey, I want to try something new, if you don't mind?" he asked almost pleadingly.

Katrina, herself wanted to try new things and was happy to oblige him. She bent over willing exposing her ass to him. His heart melted and his dick hardened as she pulled her skirt up. Her ass was beyond perfect, there was no blemishes at all about it.

Shawn, slowly caressed her ass, kneading each cheek, slipping a finger every now and again in her has and then another one in her already wet pussy. He bent over her, rubbing his hardened dick up and down her wet opening. He would enter both her holes today, but first he had to feel her mouth, lips and teeth on it. He roughly turned her around, and made her kneel down before him. Katrina, looked up as if an innocent virgin, being taught to please her master. She inched him into her mouth, slowly. His breath was caught as her mouth moved up and down on his shaft, sucking as she do so. With her hands, she massaged his sacs and he moaned at the sensation that ripped through his body. All the while she was doing these things to him, she continued to look up into his eyes.

"Play with your pussy so that it can be nice, wet and ready for me," he looked down at her as he gave his order. She willing complied.

Still sucking and stroking him, as she rubbed and searched a wet pussy for arousal. Shawn reached down, unbuttoned her two top buttons of her blouse to revealed caramel skin and beautiful brown nipples. He pulled and played with them until they were hard as pebbles. He reached down and tugged on her chin and pulled her to her feet. She was once again, turned and bent over her couches back, he slammed into her with one very swift move. His breath caught as he hit bottom. Shawn had to hold on to the couch for support, there was a sudden rush of blood that went to his head, he couldn't believe the heat and tightness that he felt in her pussy walls. He pumped slowly at first and build momentum as his passion and heat increased. She moaned in response to every stroke of his dick.

Katrina backed herself on his dick every time he pulled away from her. Shawn, started fingering her ass, this only added heat and passion to their lovemaking. She wanted him even more now. He shoved his fingers in her mouth for lubrication and she sucked on them as if they were some mysterious and delicious candy. He pushed them in her ass and she moaned yet louder.

"Hush, you don't want every woman in the office to be jealous, now do you?" he said as he slammed even deeper into her. She bit down on her lip to silence herself. "Now are you ready for me to fuck this gorgeous ass of yours?"

"Yes," she begged.

Shawn pulled out of her sweet wet pussy. As he began to enter her ass, he felt the resistance the muscles tried to put up, but they would soon lose out to their passion and desire. The deeper his dick got, the wetter Katrina's pussy, became.

"Oh Shawn, please fuck me the way I have never been fucked before."

He loved having her to beg him to fuck her. He complied with pounding and rapid strokes. It didn't take them long to orgasm and collapse in a hot pile on the couch.

"If you need to freshen up come join me in the bathroom," she said as she headed to her private bathroom, he immediately followed.

12

When Shawn returned to his office, Simone could smell the stink of sex and Katrina on him. This infuriated her even more than she thought it would. Now she really had to deal with the bitch before she lost all hope and control over Shawn.

Simone, followed him into his office, her excuse was that she had important messages to give him, which of course was not true.

"How could you be fucking that bitch, when you know you belonged to me!?" Simone hissed, as she slammed the office door closed.

Shawn was taken aback by Simone's actions. He didn't know what to say or how to react. He stood there in utter shock. 'What did she mean by he belonged to her?'

He was Katrina's mate, not hers. How dare she even speak of his Kat in that manner? The audacity of her to even approach him in this way.

"What the hell are you talking about, Simone? How dare you speak about Katrina this way?" he screamed at her.

"Don't you know I love you and that you are my alpha to my omega? Without you I am nothing. How dare you let her even touch you, knowing that we belong together?" she spoke with tears in her eyes.

Even if he wanted to, Shawn couldn't and wouldn't feel sympathy for Simone. Just the idea of being with her revolted him. She would never accept the fact that he would never want, desire nor yearn for her in any way. She didn't even appeal to him sexually. Simone was a total turn off to Shawn and even more he was on the verge of firing her.

Shawn, stormed out of his office without a word, and left Simone standing there. He had to be rid of her and fast. If he had stayed any longer in his office, he just may have killed her with his bare hands. Now, he more than understood why it was important to take extra measures to ensure his safety and that of Katrina.

Simone, had really over stepped her boundary with not just her words but mainly her actions. His first step was to go and talk to Kat, but right now he needed to calm down. He arrived so quickly at her office door that he didn't realize how furious he was and how he had let his anger fuel his movements.

He stood outside Katrina's office trying to calm down before he went in. Ava came out of the office with a notepad in her hand.

"Oh. Mr. Kenny, I was just told to call you. Please go right in, Ms. Hannah is waiting to see you." She was stunned to see him standing there looking extremely pissed. Ava was glad that anger was not directed at her, as she sat behind her desk to type the letter that Katrina had dictated to her on moments earlier.

As he stepped into her office and gently closed the behind him, Katrina, just knew something was wrong. His body movements alone told her that he was more than just upset, this was a whole other level to his anger that she was seeing. Katrina, wondered what had gone so wrong since they had made love in her office.

She went over to where he stood by her office mini bar making a drink, "Hmm... honey what's wrong?" she asked with serious concern in her eyes.

"What's fucking wrong, is my secretary going on a raving mad rampage about me making love to the woman I will be sharing the rest of my life with! That's what's fucking wrong!" he was beyond furious again and reached for Katrina. He was glad when she did not retreat but hugged him just as hard as he was hugging her.

She snuggled against his chest and asked what had Simone done that's had him acting like a raving lunatic. He took a very long, slow, deep breath before he spoke. Katrina, was beyond a borderline angry when he was done relating the story. She could see herself at this point just ripping out Simone's throat and tearing her heart from her chest, eating it as it still was beating.

"So what do you need me to do in dealing with Simone?" was her only question.

"I will handle it. She is fired immediately as my personal secretary and I will ask security to have her escorted from the building," that said he leaned down and kissed Katrina, slowly and passionately and was turning to leave when she grabbed him.

"There is one thing we need to talk about while you are here. I was thinking of turning our little trip into a honeymoon trip. Does this work for you?" her smile was the most radiant thing he had ever seen.

"Hell yes," was his response. "but first you have to meet my parents and twin sisters." This would be just one of two requests he would ask concerning their relationship.

Katrina's heart beat faster and she was happier than she had in many years. The only thing that scared her a bit was meeting his family. He sensed something changed in her and he grabbed her and kissed her again.

"Don't worry my love, they will love you just as much as I do," he whispered against her lips. With that he left her office. Now a man on a mission, he had to rid himself and this office of Simone.

She truly was a bold and blatant bitch, because he met her still in his office. Sitting like a married woman would, waiting on her cheating husband. She stood as he came in.

"Where the hell did you go? Guess you went to the bitch to get approval of me?!" she hissed between clenched teeth.

Shawn couldn't believe his ears. The foul thoughts that were possibly running through her mind, were unimaginable to him. He wanted nothing more than to be rid of her and the sooner the damn better.

"Simone, as of now your services to me and this company have now been terminated. You are to vacate your desk with all your personal belonging and security will be escorting you from the building," he then escorted her out of his office and to her former desk to collect her belongings. Two security officers were waiting to escort her from the building.

She turned on him like a wild beast, tearing at his clothing and causing a major ruckus in the office. The attention she got was not the good kind from fellow workers. They were all wondering what was going on and why would she be acting like that toward Mr. Kenny, one of the few nice guys and real gentlemen in the office. Well, whatever it was, they all agreed she deserved to be fired, and knew she wouldn't be missed. Nobody in the office really like Simone, she was tolerated but not liked.

"You and that fucking bitch will pay for what you both did to me!" Simone screamed as she was led out the building. Katrina, stood to her street side office window and watched sadly as security had to escort Simone from the building.

She always hated having to lose or fire staff members, and in this case she was both sad and elated. Should Simone had stay, who knew what would have happened next.

13

Simone, was so frustrated that she headed straight to Kevin's hotel, without calling. She needed to let off steam and anger. Kevin had proven to be an avid ally in all this, so far.

Everything was falling into place just as she and Kevin had planned. She didn't think she would have been able to argue with Shawn, but she pulled it off without a hitch. It was even better because she was angry at the fact that he had just fucked Katrina. She didn't know if she could handle seeing him with that bitch of a boss.

As she made her way up to Kevin's penthouse suite, she was recalling to memory their last encounter. The sex had been mind blowing, it was something she had never experienced before and she craved more. Simone, knew she had to tread lightly with Kevin, ally he may be but he would make a very deadly enemy.

Simone was going to be disappointed because Kevin wasn't in his room, he was at home with his visiting his pack parents, Tristram and Geneève Alexander. He hadn't seen them in almost three years, but always kept in touch.

She had no idea that for all the planning in the world, she was not going to be prepared for what was going to happen next. She arrived at Kevin's door to no avail of the knocking and ringing of the doorbell did he answer. Feeling discouraged she turned to leave, as she was about to get on the elevator, she heard a familiar voice.

'No it can't be. What would she be doing here? Is it possible she found me?' were the frightening thoughts running through Simone's head.

But the closer she got to the elevator, Simone knew it was her worst nightmare come true... Madam Keva LaRue was there, in the same hotel as Kevin. Simone knew she had to get out and fast. She took the stairs down to floors and then got the elevator and left the hotel.

Madam Keva LaRue, voodoo priestess and childhood friend to the Umbra Supreme Simone had killed, was being brought up to speed by her PI Jerome McPhee. As they got off the elevator, she could feel the presence of Simone, but she couldn't act on it, not here and not now. She would bide her time. She had come to town to meet with the lycan council and Katrina.

She would work with them to destroy Simone, before she had a chance to take any more lives. It was impertinent that Simone be stopped. With her as the Umbra Supreme, not just their communities but the world at large would be doomed.

She had passed Kevin in the lobby as she was checking in. He gave her the signal to let her know who he was. Keva knew she could never talk to him there in the hotel about their next move, especially seeing that he was working with Simone. Keva knew that what they were doing had to remain a secret until the time was right. Each step of the plan had to be timed just right in order to get the desired results.

    She went in her penthouse to rest before the meeting that evening. Keva was not just tired of all the travelling, but the deceit and double crossing that was being done to bring Simone to justice. She felt that at the end of it all her friend and 'sister' would have been proud of the way she was handling the whole situation.

    The witchcraft and voodoo communities were backing Keva in her venture to have justice met for their Umbra Supreme, Janeva Madison. They were brought up as sisters and technically they were god sisters. They mothers were best friends from childhood. Keva and Janeva were almost their mothers reincarnated for how they acted and lived with each other. Through them the truce between the communities was kept and there was peace. Up until her murder Janeva, saw to it that witches and voodoo priests and priestesses were able to live together and learn from each other.

    Her murder came as a devastating blow to both communities and when the rumors started to spread that Keva had killed her, everything went haywire. There was so much mistrust going on that Keva had to take matters into her own hands to solve her 'sister's' murder. She was happy she had hired Jerome, who was a seer. His gift was something she treasured and was happy to know he had it. With the gift, that he was born with, Jerome was able to decipher more details from those with something to hide.

    Jerome, had inherited his gift from his mom, who always knew what he was doing and with who. Now as an adult his gift helps with his job. He can not only see the present but the past and future. It has often saved his life when on a case. But this particularly case had him stumped because of the types of people involved. It was proving to be more challenging than he ever thought it would be.

14

    Keva, awoke from her nap two hours after checking into her hotel room. She was shocked to see that Jerome had not left, but instead was going over the case files. He looked up and smiled at her.

"Hope you ready for what all I have for you. This is some serious and dangerous shit we getting into," he informed her, as he passed the files to her.

Keva needed to eat, so they ordered room service as Jerome brought her up to speed on the information he had gotten from Michael Ambrose, the PI who works for Katrina. It was some gruesome things that they were learning Simone had been doing in the past five years. She had killed almost twenty people, from the time she killed Janeva to date. Most of which were males with the gift of sight or lycans, so even the more reason for them to join forces with the lycans to kill her. But that was not what Keva wanted, she wanted Simone to face a judge and jury, not to die at the hands of her or the lycan council. Even though she wanted to rip her to shreds, with her bare hands, no spells included.

Jerome sensed and saw the tension in Keva, he approached her as he always did, slow and cautiously. He had known, from first meeting her, that she was a force to be reckoned with.

"Are you sure you up for this meeting with the council tonight? Because I am sure they would allow you to rest until to tomorrow," he asked with deep concern for his client.

"No use putting it off, she needs to be stopped and soon, before any more innocents can be killed or hurt," Keva knew what she needed to do, but it would require complete privacy. "Jerome, be a darling and make a run to the bakery for me and desperately need some eclairs."

Jerome knew he was being getting rid of, he didn't mind, he needed time to think over some things. He told her it wasn't a problem and left to go so that she could have her privacy.

The minute she saw him leave the hotel through her window, Keva went to her carryon bag and took what she needed. She had to do this ritual and now, before she did anything else.

She sat on the floor in the bedroom of her penthouse. She had drawn it hundreds of times before, but she had a hard time drawing the pentagram today. Her mind was still filled with the images of carnage that Simone had left in her wake and search for the ultimate soul traveler.

'Come on Keva you have to stay focused now. This is not the time to lose sight of what you need to do,' she said to herself.

She readjusted her position on the floor, drew the pentagram. She then did her ritual, that would give her the knowledge and protection she would need to face the tasks ahead of her.

Keva knew that through it all justice for Janeva must be served, whether it be in the court system or in the law of their world. For the mystical world law was not as harsh as the world of mere mortals. While they might have been merciful to Simone for taking mortals lives, they certainly would not be for her taking the life of their Umbra Supreme.

She knew now that when her forces would be joined with the lycans, the soul traveler and the seer, it would be amplified beyond measure. This is something they were all banking on in order to finally stop Simone.

The minute her ritual was done, Jerome knocked on the door, Keva smiled, knowing he had a key why didn't he just come in. She opened the door still smiling, and so was he. She was very attracted to her PI but was great at hiding it from him. You could even say she was on the verge of falling in love with him.

Keva, had never been attracted to any man, and now she was wondering why she found this seer extremely and sensually attractive. Because you see, as a voodoo priestess, she must save herself for her ultimate warlock.

Ever since she had met Jerome, she would question herself why it was that she knew when he was nearby, how he was feeling or even what he was thinking. She was always happy to see him, no matter how bad her day was going. Jerome seemed to always know what to say and how to say it to her, whether to clarify information about the case or simply to help her feel better. Yes, she was falling for him and big time, which in her predicament could prove dangerous.

While she could bed any man she wanted, Keva, knew it would take a special man with a particular gene to give her the child, she craved to have with Jerome. She had to know and soon, how he felt about her. This would determine her what she would do after the ordeal with Simone was done.

He saw glimpses and flashes of thoughts, but nothing he could confirm or link together to make a complete thought. Jerome wasn't surprise at how she felt about him, because he had felt there was something between them from she stepped into his office.

Until recently no other woman had gotten his attention but Keva, but Katrina was fascinating. Jerome knew he would never have Katrina, for she belonged to another and it was never his place to go after another man's possession. Keva, on the other hand was not attached to anyone, but she still resisted his advances. Why? He had no idea, but he was going to find out one way or another.

Keva watched as Jerome nervously approached her. He always seemed to have nervous energy around her, or was there more to it than that. She could always feel the sexual tension between them and this time she wanted to change all that. She let him come within her personal space, loving the way he smelled as he bent down to kiss her. It was gentle at first and grew hotter and more passionate. Jerome's tongue slip passed her lips to her teeth and into her mouth, running a race between her teeth and battling with her tongue. They both moaned as they bodies grew hotter with just the thought of love making. But, it was Keva who broke the kiss. She knew she wanted him, but this would have to wait.

Jerome could no longer hide nor contain how he felt. He wanted her and was going to have her and now. He pulled her back into him, this time she bit him. He didn't care, h just kept on kissing her until she gave in. he was going to have her if only this one time. His hands were all over her as their kiss got deeper, her hands came up behind his neck. Her fingers wove through his hair, she let one of her hands slip to grip an as so firm that she had to see it. One of his hands was inside her blouse fondling her breasts, as his the other one was pulling up her skirt to feel what awaited him between her legs.

She was so wet, that he couldn't believe he had this effect on her. Their kiss deepened even more as they undressed each other. Clothes flew all over the penthouse's floor and furniture, as they were in a heated frenzy to have their bodies stripped, exposed and touching.

As he laid her on the couch, he realizes as he touches her womanhood, that she has never been with a man. He was scared and ecstatic at the same time, he would be her first and her only. He would never let another man touch her the way he was touching her now. Jerome knew he would have to take it slow and be gentle with her, so that her first time would be memorable for them both.

God she was just beautiful. Her breasts were perky and their nipples stood up, hard with excitement. Her skin was the perfect shade of mocha, her thighs and stomach were toned and extremely sexy. He gobbled her up with his eyes. Keva, just melted under the burn of his stare. She was enjoying having him look at her like this.

"This may be a bit painful for you, my amore', but I will be as gentle as I can," he whispered breathlessly in her ear.

He kissed her lips, he kissed his way down to her neck, where he bit and sucked it lightly. Then each breast was kissed and each nipple was sucked till it was hard and pebbly. Her stomach quivered as he gently bit and kissed it, sticking his tongue into her navel.

Jerome, slowed down when he got to her thighs, he gently spread her legs apart to get access to her sweet and wet mound. He licked its lips and stuck his tongue in her. She tasted like sweet honey suckle to him, and he loved it. Keva arched her back to meet his tongue as it went in and out of her. He slid a finger in her as his tongue slowly licked her clit, he gently sucked on it as his fingers went in and out on time with his tongue. He straightened, looking deep into her eyes, as he slowly and painfully entered her. She shuttered with both pain and pleasure, but she didn't stop him because she wanted him more than ever.

Jerome felt the warm blood has her maiden head was broken. Keva let out a small moan of pain, and suck her teeth into his shoulder. They moved as dancers would to a rhythm that was their own. Slowly at first and then speeding up as their passion grew. It didn't take long for Keva to climax hard around Jerome's dick, that was planted deep inside her. He climaxed not long after and she felt the heat of his cum going into her.

At that moment Keva realized that Jerome, was the man she would have a long lifetime of love with.

15

They laid there all tangled up together, Keva loved how she felt. Jerome, was the first to move, he turned and offered his hand to her. She took it and was led to the bathroom. They showered together and talked about their expectations of the meeting they were about to attend.

As she got dressed she started to feel ill, and just wanted to lay down. But, she knew she had to push pass it and go to meet with the lycan council.

"I must tell you something, Keva, as a seer I could have told you from the beginning that we are designed for just for you," he had the most gorgeous smile on his face as he spoke. "Another thing, you are not pregnant with our first child, so you have to marry when this is all over."

With that he finished getting dressed and made a few telephone calls. Keva, sat at the vanity in the bedroom, rubbing her stomach and smiling. She had always dreamed of being a mother, and from what she could tell about Jerome, he would make an excellent father. What a pair they would make as parents, a seer for a father and a voodoo priestess for a mother, she just had to laugh.

"What is so funny, mi amore'?" Jerome asked as he stepped back in the bedroom.

"Oh just the reaction of our children when we tell them what we are."

His laughter was infectious as the idea ran through his head. He wanted to tell her how they would react, because he already knew, but he kept it to himself. She looked up and joined him in the laughing.

They had to enjoy this time now, because the time was nearing for the serious business of deciding what to do about Simone. With this in mind thy left the hotel to head to the home of the lycan council leader, Tristram Alexander.

As they pulled up to the mansion, the size and the beauty of it took their breaths away, it had huge bay windows and high ceiling rooves. The structure was a mixture of brick and wood, it was just too beautiful and majestic to describe by words.

When their town car pulled up to the front door, a very tall, well-built dark skinned man opened the door for Keva. She and Jerome got out, and were told to enter the home through a massive and gorgeous designed foyer.

When they got inside, they found out that they were not the only ones there. Tristram came over and immediately started to interest them to the others who were already there. Keva was not surprised when she met Katrina, as to why Jerome had found her so attractive. If she was a man, she herself would have been smitten by Katrina's beauty.

"It is truly nice to finally meet you," Keva said ecstatically. She shook Katrina's hand, it was a strong and firm handshake.

"Indeed it is for me too," was Katrina's response, "I feel as if I already know you, because of my conversations with Jerome."

Keva was then introduced to Shawn, she understood why Katrina had taken him for her own. Keva enjoyed a brief, getting to know you, conversation with them both, and could see that they would be friends after this ordeal was over and done with. She was then formally introduced to Kevin, who was playing a pivotal role in the whole affair.

"It is my honour to meet you Madam Keva, I know that with our combined strengths we will put an end to Simone's tyranny," Kevin said bowing as he met Keva.

She felt honored meeting him as well, for with his help she knew it would be accomplished. Keva was truly thankful and grateful for their assistance in dealing with Simone.

Once the introductions were done, the group was led into a private room off from the study. There was a conference table set and everyone took their assigned seats. Tristram called the meeting to order.

Everyone knew why the meeting was called, so they went straight into it without the usual protocol. They knew with their combined information and power Simone would be ended, but they had to move and quickly. The council could not stand for any more bloodshed, whether their own kind or mortals. They had come up with a bullet proof plan to stop Simone, and Kevin was the key factor in the whole scheme of things. He had to ensure that she had no idea of what was in store for her. Kevin's role was to consistently throw her off her path and to keep her distracted as he did what he had to.

Kevin, was enlightening the council and the others, onto the facts. He told them of Simone's plan to kill Katrina in order to get her hands on Shawn. How she had tried everything to win him over, the planting of objects and the love potions, but nothing worked. Now, that Katrina had mated with him, her blood had to be split for Simone to win his affections. He told them that he was devising a plan to throw her in the wrong direction for them to corner her and let mortal man's law deal with her.

"I see you may have a flaw in your plan, Kevin," Keva spoke up. "It will take my help for you to do it, but I was thinking that I can make a powerful potion rendering her powerless. This way you would have full control over her and her thoughts."

Kevin, was about to speak again and rethought about what Keva had said. 'Mmm… the way she's thinking Keva's plan mat more than work.'

"Ok we will try it your way first and if that doesn't work then we will try it my way," he nodded in Keva's direction.

With their plans finalized, the council and its guests were invited by Tristram and his wife Genève, was invited to stay for dinner. Most stayed but some had to leave for the sake of travelling.

16

Those who remained behind, were congregated into groups. They were either discussing the meeting or in some cases how life was going. In the case of Katrina, Shawn, Kevin, Keva and Jerome, the conversation was based on family. They each spoke about their families at length, with the exception of Kevin, whom Katrina knew was adopted.

Thankful the topic was switched to love lives and marriages. Keva spoke at great lengths about the type of marriage she was going to have, Jerome never interrupted, because everything she said was true. Katrina and Shawn, sat back relaxing and enjoying the company and conversation. Kevin on the other hand wanted to leave, but was too smitten by Katrina to want to really go.

He knew from watching her and Shawn interact, that he truly would make a better mate than he would. Hands down, for as much as Kevin wanted to hate Shawn, he couldn't. he was an overall great guy and the best choice for Katrina. Kevin knew that he would never conform to who she would have needed him to be as an alpha lycan.

Kevin know realizes that all those years, he was just lusting after Katrina. He only wanted to bed her for the experience and that he could only love her as a little sister. It was now his job to protect both she and Shawn, so that the pack would remain intact. He could not afford for anyone to ruin his family, nor would he allow anyone to.

He knew he had to go, but the hated having to leave his family. Kevin kissed Katrina on the cheek and bid them all good night. His thoughts were on his next move and how he was going to continue using sex as an advantage to control Simone. He had to find a way, and fast to get her fully under his control.

Kevin knew that no potion in the world would work on Simone, plus he didn't want her following him like a love sick puppy. But, he had to do something to get the control he needed. Sex was the ultimate mechanism, and he knew how to please her.

He smelled her before he saw her. Simone, was waiting in the hotel's lobby and boy she did look upset. Kevin didn't care how she felt, to be brutally honest, he just wanted to fuck and control her.

His agenda for her would be a great fucking session, let her fall asleep and plant what he wanted to in her subconscious mind. Tonight would be a night she would never forget for as long, or as short as she lived.

Simone was furious with how things had somehow changed with the arrival of Keva LaRue voodoo priestess. She had to act and fast before Keva found her.

Even though he saw her frustration, he walked up to Simone like she was some long lost lover. Kevin smiled as he slid on the couch right next to her.

"Hey lover," he said sultrily. "Hope you haven't been waiting too long for my return?"

She stared at him like he was some unknown creature. Simone was relieved to see he was the one thing that she could surely count on. Especially, with the way things were going.

"No you didn't take too long. I was just sitting here thinking," he started to say, "but never mind that I have some stress and tension I need to work off, and you are the only person I want to work it off on."

Her smile, though beautiful, held dep dark secrets, that were deeper and darker than even he knew. Kevin stood and took her hand and guided her to the elevators. They started kissing and fondling from inside the elevator, thank goodness only they were in it.

As they got inside his penthouse, clothes were being ripped and thrown all over the floor and furniture. There was kissing biting and nibbling going on. There was no passion in anything they did, but the heat was there and a lot of it. Kevin showed no mercy as he rammed his harden cock inside her hot wet pussy. The heat was so intense that he held nothing back and before he knew it he had cum and so did she in a hot, sweaty, steamy bundle of sweaty bodies.

"Care to share with me what's gotten you so upset?" Kevin asked as he untangled from her.

She leaned up on her arm and just stared at the beauty of his naked body. She wanted more but that would have to wait, business first. Simone explained to him how she had gotten fired. She also told him that she was here to see him earlier but he was out. Simone didn't want to tell him the fear she felt when she heard Keva's voice, but for some reason she couldn't help but tell him everything.

From her fear of Keva, to the fears that her plans may backfire on her, she let everything out. Even though she felt better, Simone wasn't sure she should have let Kevin know all that she told him.

He soothed her the best way he could, but he was more than happy that she gave him an insight on how to control her. Simone's fear of just being caught, especially after all the gruesome atrocities, that she had committed.

Kevin, smiled inwardly, as he was finding ways to get her to do what he wanted and not what she desired to do. He got aroused just thinking of how he was going to use this new found instrument against her. He didn't care if her body was ready or not for him.

Kevin got out the bed pulling Simone with him, bent her at the waist on the high canopy style bed, and slammed into her.

"Brace yourself, we going to be at this for a while," she heard the change in his voice, but was not woman enough to turn around and look.

He transformation was swift, and as he changed she felt the heat from him. It was a major rush for her, she got wetter as he changed while in her. His cock became almost twice the size of any normal man, and filled every inch of her pussy. Bringing her to an early and unexpected orgasm. She didn't know if she would be able to handle it all, but she sure as hell was going to try.

He felt her body trying feverishly to keep up with his, but he had no time for pleasing her it was all about him and what he wanted. Kevin knew, that in his transformed state, he would do more damage to her. But, did he care? No, it was about his gratification not hers. This bitch think he would ever allow her to hurt or kill his fair Katrina. She had another thing coming her way, and from his point of view, it was a slow and painful death. Even though he knew the council and all concerned parties agreed not to kill her, he was going to. Her kind didn't deserve to live and be happy, while countless others suffered by their hands.

Kevin bit down on her shoulder, making sure not to break the skin and draw blood. He had no intentions, whatsoever, to make her a lycan. He just wanted to inflicted as much pain as he could to her.

Simone climaxed as Kevin bit down on her shoulder. She never knew that the combination of pain and pleasure could be such an explosive sensual act.

17

As Katrina slept in the arms of her beloved, Shawn, Keva was having a restless night. Even though Jerome was in her bed, she couldn't clear her head of the visions of the carnage left in Simone's wake. She had a spell to perform and now was as good a time as any.

She gently got out the bed and made her way to where she had drawn the pentagram earlier. The protection charms spell was easier, especially now that she knew Simone, was in the same hotel. She just had to knew if her dream was only a dream and not a full all out vision.

Keva knew that Simone would stop at nothing to get what and who she wanted. She had to make sure that Kevin would truly live up to his end of the bargain. Although she already knew he would, because of his love for Katrina and his respect and love for his pack.

Once Simone guard was down that would give him the opportunity to strike. Simone had to feel safe and secure enough with Kevin for this to happen, Keva would help this process along. With the spell in her head, she gathered what she needed from her bags, took them to the pentagram and performed the necessary spell and cast it on the charms that she had made for herself, Katrina, Kevin, Shawn and Jerome.

With charms done, she felt a little safer. As she climbed back into bed, next to a peacefully sleeping Jerome, the visions started again. Keva watched as her penthouse was transformed to a beautiful garden, filled with all kinds of exotic plants and decorated as if for a wedding, then all of a sudden the scene changed to a battle field of some sorts, where lycans and witches, along with her voodoo priestesses and priests fought side by side, against a common enemy. But she could not see who or what the enemy was, it was a bloody battle where lives and limbs were lost. The battle did not end until the enemy had been conquered. The battle field flowed red with the blood of those slain.

As the battle ended the wedding began. Lycans, witches and the voodoo societies were all represented, will a few people Keva was not familiar with. Although, they did not feel like strangers and were quite comfortable amid the crowd they were in. as she studied their face, she realizes that there are the families of Jerome and Shawn.

As the vision started to fade, she felt the weight of Jerome's leg and arm as he searched the bed for her presence. He felt her and almost immediately fell into a deeper sleep zone. Even though his breathing deepens and his body got heavier, she felt the hardness between his legs and got wet just thinking of having him inside of her again.

He slept bare back, which was her advantage. Keva began to run her fingernails slowly, gently up and down his right arm. He moaned as she ran her hands through the hair on his chest and stomach. He moaned even louder as she reached in the waistband of his boxers. She exhaled slowly as she felt his hardened cock, as it throbbed and got harder as she rubbed it. Keva leaned up on her arm and kissed Jerome's neck, shoulder and chest. She bit and sucked on each nipple making them hard as she payed attention to each one. While she was still stroking his cock, she kissed and bit her way down his chest to his stomach, the closer her mouth came to his hardened cock, the deeper he breathed.

She was at the head of things, licked it and she heard the quick exhale from him. Keva loved the idea that she could arouse him so easily. She took him slowly into her mouth, deep throating as much of him as she could. Hearing him caught between breaths, his hands playing in her hair, as she pumped up and down on him with her mouth and hand. The more she sucked him the harder his cock got and it throbbed like a heart beating inside her mouth. His moans got louder and his hands were finding and playing with her breasts, nipples and her ass as he arched his back to go deeper inside her mouth.

"Fuck man, Keva, I need to be inside you and I mean now. I can't hold out much longer," Jerome was having a hard time holding back. He needed to cum and now.

For as tempted as he was, he didn't want to cum in her mouth, at least not this time. He wanted to feel her sweet, tight, wet walls around his hard cock. She complied and got on top of him. As the head of his cock went in her pussy she gasped and slowly slid down his hard cock. She loved how he feel of him sliding in her. They moved to a drum that only they could hear. Their rhythm was a magnificent thing to see as they moved in a secret rhythm that only lovers knew. Their rhythm started slow and over time began to speed up as the passion between them build up. In no time flat they both felt the explosion that was building between them. His cock exploded inside her as her pussy milked him, as she fell forward on top of him.

"My honey love, no matter how you try, or what you do, I will never let go of you," he said as he kissed her face and then her lips.

"Oh trust me, you can get rid of me now," was Keva's response as she rolled off him to be held in his arms.

"So the future Mrs. J. McPhee, what were you doing out of bed out this ungodly hour?" His question surprised her. She didn't know how to tell him exactly what she had been doing, even though she knew he had some idea.

Keva, smiled just knowing that he was paying attention to her movements, even while he was asleep. Or so she thought he was asleep. She told him what she had been doing and why. He understood why she felt it necessary to do what she did. Jerome loved her even more as time went on, especially how she cared enough to protect himself and their new friends.

They remained in bed and watched as the sun rose to shine through the drapes in their bedroom. Cuddled up together as if they didn't have a care in the world, but knowing that they had a hard task ahead of them.

The task could prove to be a great sacrifice for all involved, especially Keva, Jerome, Shawn and Katrina. How they were going to live and have a family when everything was over? How would they help the pack to heal and rebuild? Most importantly, what would they do if they were to either lose each other or a member of their family and friends.

With these questions still racing through her mind, Shawn awoke next to her as if he had been frightened. Katrina knew he had been travelling, because of how his body stopped moving and breathing.

"We need to meet Keva and Jerome, immediately!" was the first words he spoke and with some urgency.

She got up at once and called Keva's hotel room and asked her to bring Jerome to her home immediately. She got up soon after and asked Claudette to prepare breakfast for four people, then headed to the bathroom to join Shawn in the shower.

Although he would have enjoyed haring the shower with her, now was not the time to tarry, they had business to deal with. He told her what he had seen and heard while his soul was travelling. There was a serious threat going to be made against Keva's unborn child. Katrina was shocked to hear that Keva was even pregnant.

Now she understood why Keva was so guarded around them, and why she heard a faint heartbeat when Keva was nearby. Katrina would more than fight to the death now for her new found friend. She felt that after everything was over, she and Keva would be more like sisters than just good or best friends.

Her next move would be to ask Keva and Jerome if they wanted a double wedding with her and Shawn. She felt elated hearing that Keva was pregnant and would be even happier to having to share her special day with Keva as a sister bride.

Katrina had already fallen in love with Keva and Jerome, and anyone who tried to harm them would have a serious problem with her in trying to get to them.

18

Katrina arose to the sound of Shawn's slow deep breaths. They hadn't made love the night before, but only cuddled and talked about their future plans.

How they wanted to have at least five to six kids. How they hoped that they would be blessed with Shawn's gifts and hers. How and where they wanted to live and vacation.

Now certain things became very clear to Shawn. Like why it was important to her that he loved her vacation home. How she needed his input on the way she ran her ran her companies. He was understanding even more as they talked about their future together and why it was important to her that he always be happy with decisions she made and how she lived.

She watched him as he slept peacefully next to her. The way his eyelids fluttered as he dreamed. The way he positioned his body to sleep and even the way he slept with his mouth slightly open. He even had the habit of murmuring in his sleep. All these things and more she found sexy and intriguing about this gorgeously great man that she would be spending the rest of her life with.

He must have heard her thoughts, because at that exact same moment his eyes opened, "Good morning beautiful, hope you slept as well as I did."

Katrina looked into his eyes as if into his very soul and knew she had fallen deeply and madly in love with him. She promised herself that she would do all within her power to protect him and he r new found friends.

She remembered, as a child growing up, to always live in fear of the great unknown, but now she feared the known. She had to get past her fears, to conquer them in order to live and be happy with the life she now lives. Katrina knew that with the pending danger, she would have to protect not only herself and Shawn, but also her pack.

Simone posed a great threat to her pack, and this was her major problem for Katrina, because her pack has been her family for over a hundred years. She had grown up with some and in other cases helped raise and trained others to survive. The pack that she was a part of was led by a great leader in, Tristram. He led them for almost a millennium without shedding the blood of humans unnecessarily, but blood had to be shed from time to time to protect the pack. Like now when it was most necessary to not only to protect the pack but the world at large. If Simone got her way, the world they lived in would be no more. With the aides of the voodoo and witchcraft world the lycans would be saving all mankind from sure destruction.

Katrina had a feeling that Keva was not sleeping so easy tonight knowing what was in store for all of them. Her mind kept wondering how she and Jerome were going to make after everything was over and the dust had settled. Just like Katrina and Shawn, had discussed before they had fallen asleep, in each other's arms.

19

Jerome seemed troubled and a bit upset after he hung the telephone. Keva wanted to ask what was wrong, but she waited until he sat her down and told her what the call was all about.

"That was Katrina on the phone," he began, with a weird look on his face. "She wants or rather needs us to visit her home immediately. She says that Shawn has some news that we need to hear as soon as possible."

Keva knew that Shawn may have learned something last night, after all he was a soul traveler. She prayed it was something useful to them in conquering Simone.

As they were leaving the hotel, Keva accidently bumped into a lady in the lobby.

"I am truly sorry," she started to say and then was stopped sudden when she looked directly at the lady. "Katrina, what are you doing here!"

"I am sorry; you must have me mistaken with someone else. My name is Katherine," the lady smiled in reply.

Keva mumbled her apologies and left with Jerome. Once outside she brought it to Jerome's attention how much the lady looked like their Katrina. He thought she had been mistaken, until he turned and saw the same lady coming toward them.

"You dropped this," said Katherine, as she handed Keva a handkerchief. As she turned to leave, she stopped and turned back around. "I think you mistook me for my twin sister, Katrina. I came today because I feel trouble coming her way."

Jerome and Keva both stood in shock and amazement. Without another word Katherine hugged them both and went in the hotel. They just stood there looking at her as she went in.

"Who knew? Will have to ask Katrina about her when we get there," was Jerome's response to what had just happened.

Katrina's town car and driver were waiting for them at the curb. They got in the car and silence and remained that way until they had arrived at Katrina's mansion.

Claudette greeted them at the door and led them to the study. Where both Shawn and Katrina were waiting on them. They immediately wanted to ask her about Katherine, but that would have to wait until after they heard what Shawn had to say.

Hugs, kisses and greetings were exchanged and they all sat to talk and have breakfast in the breakfast nook located in the kitchen. Once breakfast was served, Claudette left to give them complete privacy.

After eating they all went back into the study to discuss what Shawn had encounter the night before. He was pacing the room trying to find a to let them all know what he had found out.

During his night travels, he came across Simone, by pure chance, meeting with some of the people he had met at the council meeting. They were none to please to have been summons by her. Most of them, from what he had seen, didn't want anything to do with her or her plans.

Shawn started to relay what he had seen in his nightly travels with the others. They all seemed to draw the same conclusions, that Simone was blackmailing and threatening those witches, warlocks and lycans to do her biding. They had to find out who was genuinely helping her and who was being intimidated. This may prove to be a turning point in the course of things. This also explained how she was starting a step ahead of them.

Katrina told the others that it may be best that no one else was told what had been discussed. It would be better if they kept this meeting between just them for safety reasons.

"By the way Katrina, we met your twin sister in the hotel earlier," Keva said. She was stunned by the surprise look on Katrina's face. "What happen? Did I say something wrong, honey?"

"You couldn't have seen Katherine; you have to be mistaken. Katherine, has been dead for over a hundred years," Katrina said as she got up to pace the room.

"I hate to be the bearer of bad news, Katrina," every one turned as Kevin entered the room. No one heard him come in, nor had Claudette warn her mistress, that he was here. "Yes they did see Katherine."

"I had heard for years that she was granter the gift of immortality," Katrina replied. 'If this was the case, then why has she chosen to show herself now?' Katrina wondered.

As if reading her mind, Keva said that as far as she knew, twins, especially identical twins, had a connection that no one else had. And that Katherine's may have sensed the danger that Katrina was in and come to assist her in some way.

As far as Katrina knew, she never felt as if she was alone. She always thought that somehow her sister had lived as long as she had. Sometimes she even saw visions of her sister.

As all this mulled through her mind, the doorbell rang and Claudette went to answer it. She entered the study as pale as a ghost, she didn't know if she was seeing a ghost or an actually person. Claudette had been told about Katherine but there were no pictures of her anywhere. So it surprised her to see how much she and Katrina looked alike.

Katherine took her time entering the study. Shawn looked from Katrina to Katherine in utter amazement. He would have a hard time telling them apart. Katrina on the other hand walked over to her other half, and crying hugged her.

"I never knew what had happened to you. I went looking for you, but never found you," she sobbed loudly as she hugged Katherine.

20

Katherine was taken by such great emotion, that she couldn't respond right away to Katrina. They held on to each other as if for dear life. The looks that were exchanged around the room, were those of shocked, amazement and wonder. As Katherine pulled away from Katrina to get a better look at her twin sister. She was amazed at the strength she saw in her face and the fearlessness in her eyes.

"I can't believe I finally found you. Kept missing you as I searched the world over for you. Then I felt and sensed that you were in danger and I had to find you and let you know that I was alive and well," Katherine said as she kissed her little twin sister.

Katrina invited her sister to sit down and let her know what had happened to her and where she had been for more than a century.

She didn't really know where to start, but she began with the night she saw Kevin attack and change Katrina. Katherine told how she saw what had happened and ran to get help but came across a stranger in the woods. Katherine then went into how she was raped by the stranger, how she fought for her life. She wound up killing the stranger by cutting off his head. Katherine said what happen next she handle believe, she remembered everything the stranger had to other women. How he had killed a highlander and gained his wealth and knowledge.

She then went onto how she had been searching for Katrina ever since that night. Also how others had hunted her down to kill her to claim her powers and wealth. Katherine had explained how she had travelled from country to country in search of her only living sibling. She looked cross at Katrina and smiled, happily because she had finally found her.

Katherine then informed them that there was more than just Simone they had to worry about. There were immortals who wanted the powers that any Umbra Supreme can possess. These powers would modify the powers already possessed by any immortal. Katherine told them that for many years she had been in hiding because she was very good friends with both Keva and Janeva's mothers, knowing who they were and how to find them made her memories an asset to any immortal who could kill her. It had hurt her to learn that Janeva had been killed and in such a gruesome way. She told Keva she knew for a fact that she would never have killed Janeva the way the rumors were spreading about in the secret societies.

She reassured Keva that she was here to help them in any way she could. Katherine, let them all know she had gain some witchcraft powers from Keva's mother and grandmother along with those of Janeva's lineage. These spells and powers she said would prove useful in the impending battle for power in the witchcraft and voodoo worlds.

They got their head together and changed some of the plans that were discussed at the council meeting. Shawn brought Kevin and Katherine up to speed with what he had shared earlier.

Katherine agreed that this information should not be told to the council, because there could be a leak to Simone in the council. This could prove to be a bad move if this information got to the council and ruin the plans that they had for Simone. And seeing that she had people on all sides living in fear of her power, whether through blackmailing or just plain fear of losing their lives and that of their family.

21

As they all left Katrina's mansion, Katherine and Kevin got into a deep conversation about what all had happened since they had met. She gave him details that she hadn't told anyone else. She also told him that she was always attracted to him from they had first met in 1891.

Kevin invited her to have lunch with him. He called Simone and told her he had to cancel their lunch date and take her for dinner to make up for it. She was upset but she would get over it, because he had intentions to get reacquainted with Katherine.

He couldn't understand why he had gotten upset when her father had told him to marry her rather than Katrina. Kevin was puzzled as to why he never noticed the beauty that they both shared, that was now so painfully obvious now.

He opened the car door for her and asked where would she like to go for lunch. Kevin was shocked by her answer.

"Why don't we go back to my hotel room? I would love to get acquainted with you the way you were with Katrina, that night in the woods. I just won't put up as much of a fight," she had this cunning look in her eyes as she smiled.

He knew just where she was heading with this and he would love to follow her lead. Kevin gave the cabbie the address for her hotel. 'Thank goodness we aren't in the same hotel.' He thought because he knew that Simone would be there waiting on him to show up.

They barely made it into her suite, before he attacked her. Shredding her clothes like discarded rags to be thrown away. She was rammed into wall after wall as they exchanged hot, wet, and wild kisses. He was half naked when he pushed her to her knees.

"Do you want the human in me or the wolf?" he asked as he pulled his already hardened cock out for her to see.

She smiled wickedly as she looked up into his eyes as she said, "no offense the human is beautiful, but I need the wolf now!"

Her demand was met with a swift and almost painless transformation from man to wolf. He stood before her in all his magnificence. Kevin's fur was a beautiful jet black with streaks of grey like his natural hair would have been. He stood almost six feet tall on all fours, his eyes stared up at her, as if expecting her to cower or run. Katherine, did neither, but just looked at him as if he were a rare jewel she had just discovered. He slowly approached her licking and nibbling at her fingers. She knelt down before him as if to pet and stroke his lustrous coat of fur, but instead she turned and bent over for him to have full access to her already wet pussy. He sniffed her with his snout and let out a low but sexy growl. She gasped as she felt his tongue lick at her sweet wetness. Her back arched in anticipation to his tongue and teeth, so the more he licked and nibble the more she arched her back. Katherine had never experienced anything as sensual as having Kevin in wolf form lick her wanton pussy. She was begging him not to stop as she hit her first climax, but she has she was about to, he stopped and positioned himself over her.

    His weight was almost too much for her to bear, but she took it along with his massive wolfen cock as the head started to enter her. Katherine closed her eyes against tears of pain and pleasure. Her body quivered from the tension she felt between her legs and the heat of his wolf's body on top of her. The more he pushed into her, the more she was filled to limits she thought were humanly impossible. She screamed out as he hit bottom, she hadn't realized he had transformed back, so that he could be all in her. He wanted to enjoy her as a man would any woman. He kissed and bit her back, getting harder and going deeper as he did so. They started to moving to music that was being played just for them. He pulled out of her and Katherine looked around as if to ask why, but noticed that Kevin was making her turn on her side. He wanted to enter her from the back again, he lifted her leg to gain access once again to her pussy, that was dripping wet. He slid in with such ease that he gasped as he hit bottom. Them moved and gyrated as dancers would in their own private show. He pulled her hair to arch her back more so that he could go deeper and harder into her heat.

    Biting into her back, as he continued to pull her hair, he whispered in a husky voice, "You belong to me and only me. From now on you are my mate and we will mate for life."

    He came in a rush with her, just after he spoke those words. Kevin knew that from this day on he would never touch another woman the way he had just done to Katherine. He felt his seeds sliding out of her, as he pulled her to him to make promises that he knew he would keep.

    Kevin knew that when her met with Simone that night, he would be disgusted and not want to touch her. He looked at Katherine, as she molded her body to his, she was the perfect fit for him.

    Now he had another to stay and fight. He was happy that he decided to come, else he wouldn't have reconnected with Katherine nor Katrina. He was happier now that he was changing into a better lycan and even a better man. The time would soon come for him to tell Tristram exactly who he was and why he had wanted to be the pack leader.

    During his childhood, Kevin knew there was something his mother was not telling him. He just didn't know what it was. As he got older he started noticing that his father became more and more distant. He didn't want to interact with Kevin as if he was afraid of him.

He would ask his mother why it was that his father seem afraid of him. When his father was about to die, he called Kevin into his bedroom. He told Kevin the story of how he had married his mom to save the both of them. How they were cared for by his paternal grandmother. He was told how his grandmother never wanted his mother to tell his biological father that he had a son. Who would be the rightful heir to his estate and title.

Little did Kevin know how much of a major role he would play in his father's business. When he turned eighteen, his mother took him to a man, who lived in a mansion, and told him that this man would train him how to use his gifts wisely. The man was Tristram, and his mother had never told him that Kevin was his son.

Like clockwork every time there was to be a full moon, she would take him there. He was taught the art of transforming faster than most lycans, because he was born one and not turned. He had stronger intuitive and senses powers than the others he trained with. Kevin was even stronger at persuasion than Tristram was, which he loved.

22

Tristram was driving his wife, Geneve, insane with all the pacing he was doing. He needed to find out why it was that Simone had killed two of his best lycans and why. These questions he needed to have answers to and he knew just who to call.

He answered on the fifth ring, "Kevin I need to see you and now please."

Kevin hated leaving her but he had to see what was so urgent for Tristram to be calling him and sounding desperate. He felt right away that something was wrong, and needed to find out. He could hear from the sound of the older man's voice that something was seriously wrong.

"Darling, I really hate leaving you like this, but I have to go," he said kissing her lightly on the cheek, while he fondled her exposed breast.

Smiling Katherine said, "I understand duty calls."

He leaned in once more before he got dressed and whispered, "I hope it's not a problem, because we didn't use any form of protection."

Katherine's laughter filled the room. "No need to, I can't get sick not can I get pregnant." He kissed her again, deeply this time and turned and got dressed.

He was still smiling as he left her hotel, wondering what would be Katrina's reaction to him falling in love with her sister. Kevin doubted she would be angry, upset not hurt. She would be happy for them both, who knows there may even be a double wedding when everything was over and done. Little did he know there would be a triple wedding.

It didn't take him long to get to Tristram from Katherine's hotel, even though the ride was relatively short, he had a lot running through his mind. Mainly what had rattled their leader to the point that he was shaken.

As his cab pulled into the driveway, he noticed Tristram at once waiting outside for him along with Michael. Now he knew it was something very serious that they were dealing with. They greeted him as soon as he exited the cab and asked him to walk with them through the gardens.

"It is vital that what we tell you, remain within this group of just the three of us. It was brought to our attention that last night a few lycans were killed and not just any lycans either. Two council members and their bodyguard. These were the ones who brought Simone's actions against lycans to our attention," said Tristram gravely.

Michael produced an envelope containing the photos of the scene and there were more gruesome than the ones for the murder of the Umbra Supreme. There was blood every way, as if it was a slaughter house. Dismembered limbs were thrown all over the floor, as if they were cut off and then just tossed about, like discarded old rags. It was something out of a badly written horror movie.

Kevin searched the faces of Tristram and Michael for any sign of who or what may have done this. They only looked at him blankly in response, because they had no idea how it had happened. But they had some idea as to who was responsible for it. The both of them knew it had something to do with the council meeting and Simone, but how would they connect the two. This was where Kevin's role came into play.

He knew from their expressions that he would have to do the unthinkable tonight with Simone. Kevin knew he had no choice in the matter, he had to protect the pack at all cost.

He had to find a way to fuck Simone without her knowing about Katherine. He told them he would handle it the best way he could and get back to them as soon as possible.

Kevin left Tristram and Michael still talking in the garden. His first stop would be to Katherine; he was sure she would have a spell to protect him from Simone. That and, he needed to tell her what he must do. He prayed she would understand, that it was not his desire to be physically close to Simone.

Katherine opened her suite room door before he had a chance to knock. She pulled him into her in a long sensual embrace and kissed him slow and very passionately. Kevin was stunned when she released him.

"What did I do to deserve all that?" he said flustered.

"Just had to give you some reassurance that I love you. I already know what has been asked of you to do. She may get your body tonight but, I will always have your heart," she said as she sashayed away from him. "Follow me, I have missed something to protect you from her and to throw my scent off you."

He stood stunned, 'How did she know he was coming here just for that?' he wondered as he walked over to her.

"We have linked and exchanged some essences when we made love earlier today. So now I am mentally and physically linked to you. So you see what you hear, feel and sense, I do as well. It's the gift and curse with mating between an immortal and a lycan."

Kevin just stood there smiling and looking at this amazing woman, that he can and already claimed as his own. He now had more than just the pack to make sure that their plans went off without a hitch.

He drank what she the potion she had made to protect him. Then he stripped as she instructed him to. He then went in the bathroom, she told him he had to get into the tub. She then bathed him down in a sweet but powerful potion, this would throw her scent off of him and enable him to fuck Simone royally and without a conscientious.

23

Kevin went to kiss Katherine, but she wouldn't allow him to. He had to remember he had to remain clear and clean of her scent. He sighed in desperation and left her blowing kisses at him through the elevator doors.

He stepped into the lobby of his own hotel less than twenty minutes later, and low and behold Simone was waiting for him in the lobby.

"Where have you been all day?" she demanded of him.

He smiled and continued to head to the elevators. When they were in the elevator and alone, he grabbed.

"Oh my dear, precious Simone, where I have been does not concern you, nor what I have been doing. What does concern you however is what I and about to do to you," he grabbed her and pulled her roughly to him. Pushing a hand under her dress he realizes she has on no underwear, oh how he did appreciate it how she paid attention to what he liked. He bent her over right there in the elevator and stopped it. He was hard but not for her, but his beloved Katherine. Kevin was envisioning that she was Katherine, and that this would be their first time fucking in an elevator. He lifted her dress over her head and entered her mercilessly, with no warmth and no love, he pounded his hardened cock deep inside her already soaked pussy.

He took him less than ten minutes to cum. He didn't care if she was satisfied or not, he just tossed her aside like an old rag doll. He was done with her and no longer wanted her in any way. He wanted nothing more than to rip her throat out and watch her suffocate on her own blood. Kevin had to reel in his anger, because he could feel his transformation start and he had to get it under control and fast. He still needed her to live so he can learn what he needed to from her.

Simone looked back at Kevin all heartbroken, feeling used and useless. The way those lycan had possibly when she killed them and drank their blood. The more of their blood she drank the more power she felt and it did help to heighten her senses to know when someone was using or lying to her. But for some reason she could never read or sense what Kevin was thinking or feeling. All she did know was that he may not be her mate, she craved and yearned to always have him inside her. Simone, was wondering what spell he had used on her to get her so addicted to him. He was a drug that she had to have every day and as many times in one day as possible. As the elevator came to stop at his penthouse floor, she felt herself being led forcefully into his penthouse.

"Get naked," he said in a rough almost inhumane voice. He had transformed just enough to have another big hard on to fuck her once again with.

He had no love for her nor did he admire or lust after a needy woman like Simone. All of the qualities she displayed, he hated in women. She was weak and before he was done with her she would be even weaker.

Kevin vowed to himself that she would pay for everything she had ever done to those he loved. He would spend his life if he had to, destroying her and everything she stood for. He was tempted to just have his way with her and be done with it, but he had to bide his time and get what he needed out of her first.

Simone was scared for the first time of the power that Kevin wheedled over her. She hating that he could make her do whatever he wanted at the drop of a hat. She never wanted any man to have this type of power over her, but she couldn't resist Kevin in any way.

"Why aren't you done yet?!" he was demanding of her. "Get on the floor and assume the position a dog would, to receive your punishment. Now!"

Simone did as she was told. He stood in front of her, with a hardened cock in his hand. He was partially transformed, and in this state his cock was three times the size of the average one. She knew he had all intentions of inflicting as much pain as he could possibly do to her. Simone wondered what she had done for him to react to her the way he was now.

Kevin roughly shoved his hardened cock in her mouth, "And you better not bite down on it. Suck it as if your life depended on my cumming in your mouth."

He began pumping in and out of her mouth, "Now that you are truly my bitch, look up and let me see into your eyes."

Simone complied with tears in her eyes, the tears only made Kevin want to hurt her even more. 'How dare she shed tears after all the lives she had already taken and would take if I don't stop?!' was running through his mind, as he rammed his cock as deep as it would go in her mouth. Simone was gagging in the sheer size of the cock alone. It wasn't just thick, it was long and throbbing, all this made it harder for Simone not to bite down on him. He shoved even harder and she began to sob, this accelerated his blood even more.

The more she cried, the harder and bigger his cock got. Kevin was watching as the corners of her mouth started to rip, but he didn't care, he was enjoying hurting her. He pulled out of her mouth and bent her over the nearest sofa. Kevin slammed into her amazingly wet pussy with a movement so swift she hadn't expected it. She screamed for the pain and he could smell the blood that was draining down the insides of her thighs. He smiled cunningly knowing that she was in serious pain, but wasn't woman enough to make him stop. He felt as he pushed passed her cervix walls into her wombs.

"If I were you I would stop the water works, because I just getting started on you. When I am done no man will want or even look at you," he snarled, still seeing all the carnage from the photos he was shown earlier.

He pulled out of her and rammed his cock in her ass, she screamed even louder than before. Kevin, honestly didn't care how much pain she was in, she would be dead and soon. Just as that thought popped in his head, he heard Katherine's voice, 'She must not die like this. She must pay for her crimes and through the proper channels.' He let out a low growl and transformed to his full human form. Kevin knew he had to respect the wishes of not just the lycan council, the voodoo and witchcraft societies, but especially the love of his life, Katherine. He pulled out of her and let her fall to the floor, as if she were dead.

"Get the fuck out of here, before and have no mercy on you. I have all intentions right now to rip your throat and tear your heart from your chest and eat it," his gaze was spiked with hatred and blood.

She gathered herself together, but did not leave. Simone had all intentions of finding out from Kevin, why he had treated her the way he did tonight. Was there another woman? Or did he smell the blood of the lycans she had killed, on her still?

Simone stepped timidly toward him, as an abused child would go to an abusive parent. Head held low and staring at the floor, she asks him, "Why did you do what you just did to me? I didn't deserve that. Is there someone else, have you found your mate?" She was sobbing as she asked these questions of him.

"You have no right to question me, in any way. After all you were just a toy to play with and now that I am bored with you, its time you left," he turned away from her. "Now it's time I wash your stench off of me. Good bye, Simone."

His last words were like a dagger stabbing her deep in her heart. All Simone could do was to stand there crying and pleading with Kevin. He looked at her in disgust and went in the bathroom without another word.

She was too afraid to leave and even more afraid to stay. He may just kill her if he met her still standing there crying. She got the rest of her belongs and left. Crying and vowing that this would not be the last time he would lay hands and eyes on her.

She vowed to herself that she would find a way to hurt him the way he had hurt her. This was far from over, while she still needed him to finish what they had started, he would still pay. Maybe, even with his very life.

24

Simone knew within herself that, while yes she still needed Kevin, he would die when she got Shawn to be hers. She needed to meet with the others and now. She had grown weary of waiting on the right time. The right time was now, while they thought she wasn't capable of doing anything. She took her cell out and made the calls she needed to.

"Get all the things together. We doing this tonight and I mean right now!" she hung up and flagged down a cab.

Just as she entered her apartment, her telephone began to ring. It was the lycan whose wife she held prisoner. He had called to let her know that everything was ready at the spot they had decided to strike from. She told him that she would be there in under fifteen minutes.

Simone went in her bedroom and prepared her body for the battle she knew was eminent. She made the potions and did the spells necessary for power and protect, but as she was preparing so were Keva and Katherine.

Jerome had given them the heads up that Simone would attack tonight and it would be very close to home. He told them that she intended to attack Tristram and Genève, whom she thought to be the weakest of all the lycans and closest to Katrina. He also told him, in confirmation to what they had discussed, was that the lycans she had working with her, were being blackmailed and that she had their families held hostage but he couldn't see where yet. He went back in the bedroom to tune into the whereabouts of the hostages, this way they could release them and regain the stronghold over Simone.

Simone, was startled by her cell ringing. 'Who in the world would be calling me know?' was the question that ran through her head. She answered after the sixth ring, not really wanting to answer it.

Surprisingly, it was Kevin, apparently calling to apologize for his behavior earlier. Saying that he had no idea what had come over him, and that he was consumed with the thoughts of her being with Shawn, and no longer wanting or needing him. He felt jealous and betrayed because she didn't want him but Shawn. He even told her how he felt she was using him and would kill him when she was done with him.

Simone mulled all this over and was thinking that she would definitely have to kill Kevin by the end of the night. After all she would have Shawn, and have no more use nor need for Kevin. Plus, he now proved to liability rather than an asset.

Simone got dressed and left her apartment, unknowingly being watched. She moved so swiftly that they almost lost her as she walked the streets. She was a woman with a purpose and on a mission to destroy all her enemies and her allies. There would be no one left one left to challenge her when she was done, she would see to that.

She told him that she was ready to deal with all the lycans if she had to in order to get Shawn. Which Kevin knew meant him as well. He told her he would meet her where they had arranged to get things started. He remembered that they were to meet at the park across from Tristram's mansion.

The park offered cover from them being seen. It would only take Kevin ten minutes to get there is he walked from his hotel. Has he prepared to leave, he made one very important call without using a telephone. Kevin positioned himself on the floor and channeled all his energy to reach Katherine. It was amazed at how fast she responded and that it had actually worked. He informed her about the actions that were to be taken that very night and where it would start. He told her to tell the others but to doing it by going o Katrina's, because they were already there. Katherine, cautioned him to be extra safe and to guard against his emotions or else Simone would be able to read him. Their link was broken by Katherine, right after she told him that she loved him.

He arose off the floor and quickly got dressed to head to meet Simone and the others. Within ten minutes of leaving his hotel he arrived at the designated spot in the park. The others were gathered in a circle and had already started the ceremony that would transform Simone to look, act and talk like Katrina. This had to be done for her to gain entrance into the mansion, but what they had failed to tell Simone was that she would still carry her own scent. They knew that this would be her downfall, even though they were in fear of her, she had to be killed for the safety of all concerned.

While this was going in the park, Keva had located the families that Simone had held hostage. She informed Jerome who in turn passed the message on to Tristram via mental telepathy, and told him that they had to act fast.

Tristram sent a group of his lycans along with a few witches, that were staying at his mansion to get the families to safety, as the others who were there prepared for the arrival of Simone and her unwilling minions. The perimeters were secured and the security at the gates were on the lookout for Simone and the others.

Katrina, Shawn, Jerome and Keva were told to stay put until they were needed. They hated not being at the center of what was going on, but they understand and complied with Tristram's orders. He had his wife, Genève, taken some place safe and out of harm's way. He had all of the senior council members, that were unable to fight, sent where his wife was. Once they all were safe, he prepared himself to fight, something his wife nor Katrina wanted.

Katherine had finally arrived at Katrina's around two am, and met them all preparing to leave at a moment's notice. She helped Keva with potions for healing and protection, as the others gathered weapons from Katrina's basement.

"Whoa, lil sis, what type of arsenal you have down in that dungeon of yours?" Katherine asked as she saw them bring up rifles, shotguns, grenades and hand held fire arms.

Katrina, only laughed at her big sister, knowing that she would never be able to explain how she got such weaponry and more down in her basement. She didn't reply, but went right on loading guns with silver bullets, that had been sleeping in potions from the night before. She felt happy and sad at the same time, Katrina, prayed that all those she loved would live through the night to celebrate her wedding day with her.

Katherine sensed this and went over to hug and give her a light kiss on the forehead. At this the others realized that this may be their last time being together. There were hugs and kisses exchanged all around Katrina's kitchen.

Katrina let them know that they would not be using their own vehicles, but the trucks and vans that were sent over by Kevin's company. This was so that they could move through undetected by Simone.

"Ok guys and girls let's show this bitch who's really in charge around here. Keva now is the appointed hour to reach Kevin and then Tristram." Katrina said as she pulled her duffel bag onto her shoulder, even though it was very heavy she carried it as if it was nothing more than a regular handbag.

They paired up, Keva and Katherine went in the truck, Jerome and Shawn took the van and Katrina went in the other smaller truck. As they drove out Katrina's driveway, they went in separate directions, because they knew the house was being watched.

As they drove, each noticed that the men, in the car parked outside Katrina's mansion, looked confused and didn't know who to follow. They decided to follow the last vehicle to leave and that was Katrina. This was a part of their plan, and they took the bait whole heartedly.

Katrina took her followers on a mini wild goose chase, before doubling back to her home. As she turned in her drive way so did they.

'Wow, they truly are bold in following me all the way into my driveway.' She thought as she got out of the truck and headed toward her garage. Once inside the garage, she positioned herself to hit the first one. Just as he entered the garage he was clubbed to sleep, while Jerome hit the second one just outside the garage's door. Because, the others just like Katrina had doubled back to her mansion. They gagged and tied both men.

Katrina, stripped them of their guns, knives and cell phones. With this done they all left to head directly to Tristram's mansion. Thankfully they arrived a few minutes later undetected by Simone and her minions.

Kevin sensed that both Katherine and Katrina were with Tristram, and he linked his mind with that of his love Katherine.

'We are just about ready to send in Simone. Be ready because not long after she is allowed entrance the attack will begin. I love you.'

Messaged sent he moved into the inner circle and strategized with the others.

They positioned themselves to see Simone gain access and then entrance to the mansion. Once she was inside, their moved quickly to their attack positions.

Simone was told to wait in the study for Tristram, because he and Genève had retired early. She paced the study as she waited, wondering why it was taking him so long to get to her. Simone had assumed that once she used Katrina, Tristram would not resist running to her aide.

25

Attack positions taken and defense positions taken, both sides were ready to fight to the death for what they believed in or in fear of losing their families. Everyone was doing what they felt was best at this time.

The lycans that had been sent by Tristram to get the hostages, contacted Keva to let them all know that they had gotten all of them out. And, that they were safe with Genève. Keva relayed this message to the others and this was the advantage they needed over Simone.

"Do you think you can link with those outside? Please let them know that their families are safe and should they still choose to fight with Simone, they will be killed along with her," Tristram asked.

Keva's response was remarkable to say the least, "Do you think of me as a second rate magician? I thought you wanted me to do something more challenging."

After Keva did this it was now time for Tristram to make his way to the study to meet Simone, disguised as Katrina. He rushed in the study as if he had a gunman running behind him. He came to an abrupt stop as he stepped into the study, and just watched as Simone was pacing back and forth in his study. He waited until she realized he was in the room.

"What's wrong my child?" he asked her with a fatherly concern.

"I don't' know if I am capable of protecting both I and Shawn, should Simone come for him," she ran to him sobbing, with fake tears in her eyes. "I am not sure that he is strong enough to resist her." She was playing her part very well indeed.

Tristram took a step back and made her sit down. He bided his time while she, supposedly, composed herself to continue talking. She ranted on about how strong Simone and the people following her were getting, and all the information they were gathering against all of them.

Tristram reassured her that he would never let no harm come to her nor Shawn. She looked up at smiling, with blood and ferociousness, as she took the silver knife from the waist band of her pants. She wasn't fast enough, because out of nowhere Katrina grab her arm, forcing her back into the chair she was sitting in.

A ravish struggle ensued between the two women, during which Katrina partially transformed. Simone proved to be stronger than she figured she would be. It seemed to Katrina that the more she fought with Simone, the stronger Simone got. Then she realized that she had been stabbed with the knife and was losing a lot of blood and fast. The wound was a long and deep gash under her left breast. She howled in pain as Simone drove the knife even deeper in the wound.

Shawn came from out of nowhere and grabbed Katrina from Simone's clutches, as Tristram in turn grabbed Simone. She was really putting up a serious fight with Tristram. She would not allow herself to be taken prisoner by these animals, she was after all the Umbra Supreme.

She would play on their compassion for Katrina, by pretending to act like Katrina. She begged Shawn to let go of the imposter pretending to be her. Simone then turned to Tristram with watery pleading eyes begging him to recognize her as the real Katrina. But, to all avail she failed, because she didn't have Katrina's scent.

"Can you really believe this bitch?!" Kevin appeared from out of nowhere. "Do you really believe that we can't smell you for who truly are?"

Just as he began to transformed some of the security guards came in the study to inform them that some of Simone's followers were still attacking the mansion.

"Take her and carry her downstairs and lock her ass in the basement," Tristram commanded as two of his bodyguards also had entered the room. "Take her over to chair and let's have a look at her wound."

Shawn complied and gently laid Katrina on the couch. Tristram gingerly lifted her shirt to access the injury. It was a very deep and gaping gash that was about an inch in length and it was bleeding profusely. They had to get her to their doctor on call but right now that would have to wait, they had a bigger problem on their hands.

Tristram asked Jerome where Keva was. He told Tristram that she was up in the attic trying to fully connect with all the minds of Simone's followers. She sadly was not successful because some were able to block her out, and those she did connect with didn't believe that their families were safe. So a bloody battle was ensuing on the grounds of Tristram's estate. He had to do something or else all hope was lost along with a lot of lives.

He called for the lycans who had secured the families to bring them to the estate at once. He was questioned by them as to why they should do such a thing seeing that it was so dangerous there.

"I know you may think I am being foolish and irresponsible with their lives, but it must be done in order to save everyone."

"Ok as you wish sir," was all the response he got from the lycan in charge there.

Michael came into the study letting them know that Simone had someone escaped from the body guards. She had used some sort of potion to get them to do her bidding and was now somewhere within the mansion. He had security searching for her as they spoke. Tristram had to make sure that Simone was caught and dealt with. She would be an uncontrollable force if she was allowed to escape.

26

Tristram's first move was toward the attic to talk to Keva and see if she had made any progress. When he got there, she was in the middle of the floor chanting a spell under her breath. He hated to disturb her, but he was left with no other choice.

"I really hate stopping you, but I need you to change the message. Let them know that their families are on their way here," Tristram told Keva, confident that she would do her endeavor best to get the message across.

All she did was look at him with a big grin on her face, happy to oblige in any way possible. She repositioned herself on the floor and began chanting again but the words were different.

Tristram step toward a window facing the west entrance to his estate. He was heartbroken to see his own family fighting amongst themselves, and all the carnage that was being left behind. His estate resembled and ancient battlefield. There were bloody bodies and bodies all the place. What was once his wife's beautiful garden, was now a living graveyard, with wounded lycans, witches and voodoo priestesses and priests. Some were so close to death that they were begging to be killed, others missing body parts that were either nearby or in some other part of the estate. Those whom had died during the first wave were being trampled upon like nothing more than mere garbage.

He couldn't take the site anymore and was about to turn from the window, when he saw her, Simone was walking through the fighting, as though she was out on a nightly stroll of the gardens. He had to alert the others that she was headed toward them in the study.

He ran downstairs and was just in time to see her enter the study through a side door. No one else in the room had seen or heard her come in. he immediately alerted Michael, who was nearest to her, but she cast him aside like a child's toy. Next was Shawn, she didn't want to harm him, because she still needed him, so she threw some sort of powder in his face. He fell to the floor howling and scratching at his face. Tristram transformed and charged at her, but she was ready for him too. He got shot with a mini gun that she had custom made just for this occasion. As Simone had incapacitated all of them, she made her way to Katrina, who laid helpless on the couch. The closer she got to Katrina the bigger her grin and the wilder her laugh got. She was finally going to kill this bitch once and for all.

"You really thought, you would end up with my alpha? Darling, you so underestimated me and my capabilities. Nothing and no one will ever come between Shawn and I. again!" Simone dove toward Katrina, but unbeknown to her, Katrina was no longer on the estate.

Katherine, stood up just as Simone was about to lunge the silver dagger, in whom she thought was Katrina.

"Bitch you are sadly mistaken for messing with my twin sister. Now you will have me to deal with," Katherine grabbed the dagger from Simone's had, when she was shoot in the heart.

Katherine clutched ate her chest, as if on her dying breath and looked at Simone in stupid surprise. Simone stood over her as she dropped to the floor. She knelt over her to shoot her again, but sorry would be her cry, because Kevin was running toward them both. He was transforming as he neared Simone.

"Do you really believe you would get away from me this time? You end is at hand and there is no one to stop me this time," he said between growls.

She fired the gun and him but to no avail it was out of bullets. He circled her, as if hunting his prey. Kevin stood on his hind legs totally transformed, and began to rip her skin and then limbs off, one by one. He watched the surprised shock on her face.

"I am not going to die tonight as you had planned to kill me, but you surely will meet your make and soon."

Before she had chance to react Kevin was on her. First he ripped out her heart and began eating it while it was still beating. The last image Simone had was of Kevin eating her heart, because after that he ripped her head clean off her body. Simone's carcass dropped to the floor in violent convulsions.

With Simone's blood on him, Kevin ran to see how Katherine was doing. She sat up smiled sadly at him saying, "she left you no choice but to kill her."

She fell forward in his arms weak from the blood she loss. Tristram got to his feet and so did Michael.

"I do believe they have all stopped fighting," Michael said, as he listened to the quiet stillness from outside the walls of the mansion.

The battle had ended, most families were reunited, but sadly for some, they would have to bury their dead. But all in all there was not that many in terms of loss of life.

A few days later with all the dead buried there was caused for celebration. Kevin and Katherine, Jerome and Keva, along with Shawn and Katrina, all tied the knot on the same grounds that blood was split in a battle that should not have happened. It was truly a beautiful and glorious occasion. Each bride had their own distinct taste, flare and fashion to their wedding dresses. Katherine wore an ancient bridal grown from her era in the colors of cream and gold, decorated with diamonds and jewels from her own personal collection. Keva wore a teal and gold colored dress, adorned with jewels handed down through different generations of her mother's family. Katrina, just had to go all modern with a beautiful coral colored dress with jewels and gems with the colors of the sea.

After their vows was exchanged, Katrina invited them down to her island retreat that she had bought. Their honeymoons would be like non other. She told Tristram and Genève, that they were coming too, after all they did deserved a vacation after their ordeal.

No one put up any objections to her invitation. They left that very afternoon in her private company jet.

They all marveled at the beauty of the islands as they approached her cay. It was truly a gorgeous aerial sight as they all saw her island estate. It was boarded with native fruit trees and the mansion itself was an architecture's dream. It had tiles rooves and towers, like those on the castles of days of old. The sidings were made of clay brick and cider blocks in the colors of flamingo pink trimmed in white. With shutters of white and pink, each door was arched in style and floor to ceiling in height. Indeed, it was a beautiful sight to see.

She sighed and laid into her husband's loving arms, for she was now and always would be a she wolf in paradise.

Made in the USA
Columbia, SC
13 October 2024